Donated 11/22

CARVEL

THE CHRISTMAS CAT

— •◆• —

A NOVEL

JOHN S. LITTELL

SOURCEBOOKS LANDMARK™
AN IMPRINT OF SOURCEBOOKS, INC.®
NAPERVILLE, ILLINOIS

This publication is designed to provide accurate and authoritative infor-
mation in regard to the subject matter covered. It is sold with the under-
standing that the publisher is not engaged in rendering legal, accounting,
or other professional service. If legal advice or other expert assistance is
required, the services of a competent professional person should be
sought.—*From a Declaration of Principles Jointly Adopted by a Committee
of the American Bar Association and a Committee of Publishers and
Associations*

Published by Sourcebooks, Inc.
P.O. Box 4410, Naperville, Illinois 60567-4410
(630) 961-3900
FAX: (630) 961-2168
www.sourcebooks.com

Library of Congress Cataloging-in-Publication Data

Littell, John S. (John Smith)
  Carvel, the Christmas cat / by John S. Littell.
    p. cm.
  ISBN 1-4022-0048-X (alk. paper)
  1. Cats—Fiction. 2. Brothers and sisters—Fiction. I. Title.
PS3612.I87C37 2003
813'.6—dc21

                                                    2003004764

Printed and bound in the United States of America
BG 10 9 8 7 6 5 4 3 2 1

For Steve and Sue

AUTHOR'S NOTE

Although this is a novel, it is based on a true story—a story of love, redemption, and the power of Christmas to heal a wounded heart. It is also about a kitten named Carvel. How we came to acquire a cat—and lose her—involves a quarrelsome old woman, a paper-thin tire, a milkshake (chocolate), and a little girl's perfect faith. Had any one of these ingredients been absent, there would have been no cat and no story to tell. Fortunately, all of these elements came together on a freezing December afternoon in 1962.

Because this is a work of fiction, all the names have been changed—except the kitten's. Somehow, I don't think Carvel would have minded.

PROLOGUE

The kitten quivered with cold and fear and hunger. She was only six weeks old, but she was forced to fend for herself in the cruel winter weather. Though she tried with all her might to live, she was losing the battle. The survival instinct in her was strong, but like all cats she had to be taught how to hunt and forage and she had never known a mother. Her only memories were of being kicked and tortured by a boy who had kept her penned up in a wooden crate encrusted with her own filth. Every day he would bring her what was left in a carton of milk and toss it at her, laughing when it hit her head. While she tried desperately to lick the meager contents of the paper carton, he would begin poking her with a stick—hard. She cried, begging him to stop, but that only made him laugh louder and strike her more viciously.

Sometimes he would burn her with matches, lighting them and dropping them on her matted fur, causing her to shriek in terror. The smell of phosphorous made her tremble with uncontrollable panic. Other times he would pick her up and talk softly to her, making her relax. Then he would fling her high in the air and she would land with a bone-cracking crunch on the cement floor of the abandoned garage where he kept her.

"Always on her feet," the boy would say and do it over and over again until she went limp and no longer tried to protect herself. She didn't know why he hated her so or why he took such pleasure in hurting her, she just knew that the milk carton he brought kept her alive.

Then one day, she heard a rough deep voice that she knew didn't belong to the boy and she began to meow.

"What the hell?" the man said. "Get out of there and go home."

He overturned the filthy box and she limped as fast as she could to get away from him before he did something terrible to her. The problem was she had no home to go to, no one to care for her and love her.

Painfully, she moved as best she could on her twisted left front leg, but it had snowed and the ground felt like fire on her soft pads. She started down a hill, going toward the smell of something—something that might be food. When she reached the bottom of the hill, she saw two buildings, one with giant golden arches in front and the other with an enormous ice cream cone on top. She didn't know what these buildings were, but she could smell the tantalizing aroma of what she hoped was something to eat. Sneaking warily around the perimeter of the two buildings, avoiding the humans, she found part of a hamburger wrapped in greasy paper. She sniffed it with her dirty nose, then pounced on it and devoured it.

Feeling more confident, she searched for something more to eat. That was when she saw a large animal of some kind. She knew from experience to fear humans, but she was curious about this black-and-tan creature that was walking toward her. Showing no fear, she hobbled slowly to meet it. The creature ran at her with lightning speed and seized her in his slobbery jaws. His sharp pointed teeth dug into her flesh as he picked up her slight weight and shook her with all his great strength.

"Bingo!" a man yelled. "Put that down. It's dirty."

The Doberman obediently did as he was told, leaving her stunned and bleeding on the cold pavement of the parking lot.

"What's wrong with you?" the man said. "You'll catch a disease or something. Let's go."

With the little strength that was left in her, the kitten dragged herself into the bushes at the back of the building. When she got there, she lay panting on the frozen ground, her skin lacerated, her bones aching and throbbing, and her heart beating wildly. For more than an hour, she fought off death, never once thinking about what she had to live for. She was just an insignificant little kitten. Her life or death would not matter to anyone—not even to herself.

As the sun began to set, an icy wind blew over her, making her shiver. She felt terribly tired, and she wanted to sleep. But suddenly there was a smell she recognized, the smell of milk. She raised her head from the ground and saw something that was familiar—a paper cup. Even in her forlorn state, there was a certain spark within her that still burned. She was curious.

With excruciating slowness, she inched her way toward the cup and pushed her nose inside. At the back of the cup, the dregs of a chocolate milkshake provided moisture to her parched tongue and the sides of the cup protected her from the biting wind. It was a tight fit, but it was as good a place as any to die.

Part I

December 15–17, 1962

Part I

Chapter 1

Old Lady Langley was a crank, to begin with. There was no doubt whatsoever about that. A vexing and contentious woman, she had drained the joy from many of my childhood days and delighted, I thought, in destroying my pleasure in playing endless innings of softball. In fact, the Curse of Langley had descended upon me during the summer of my ninth year when softball was banned from the playground forever—all because Miss Langley lost a few windows. It was all her fault, of course. I couldn't help it if she lived along the left field line. Errant pop flies automatically found their way to her kitchen windows as if drawn there by some invisible force. After the ball had made a satisfying shattering sound upon impact, there would be a scream of outrage as Old Lady Langley roared incoherently through the hole in her glass. Rather than face her wrath, every kid on the playground would take flight immediately.

Running was futile, however, because Miss Langley always knew who had done the deed. Either she had built-in miscreant radar or she was secretly monitoring the game with hawklike intensity from her aerie high above the playground. The offender's parents would receive an irate phone call from Miss Langley, one that came with insults, demands for payment, and threats of multiple lawsuits. The parents of the players, as parents are wont to do, banished softball from the playground that summer, citing Miss Langley's inalienable right to intact windows. We kids adjusted, but we hated Old Lady Langley with a fervor unmatched in the annals of childhood.

Seven years after the Great Softball Expulsion, I still hated her, but I was perched precariously high on a freezing aluminum ladder, attempting to sling a string of Christmas lights around one of her fir trees.

The idea wasn't mine. It was my mother's. Every year at Christmastime, Mom would suddenly become suffused with the holiday spirit. The transformation was astounding. Normally, my mother was a practical soul who believed that charity began at home and that the South Sea Islanders and starving Armenians should take care of themselves. However, around the middle of December, she would be seized by the desire to be a more caring person. I don't know if Mom was visited by ghosts, but she would wake up one morning brimming with love for her fellow man.

"Here we go again," my father would sigh at the breakfast table, spotting the faraway look in her eyes.

The whole family dreaded this moment because we knew that Mom's idea of helping the helpless meant sending her children and husband off on various acts of charity. As far as I can remember, she never actually did any good deeds herself. She was the director of good deeds; the rest of us were charged with making her philanthropic dreams come true.

"I spoke with Miss Langley yesterday," Mom told me as

I cringed over a bowl of Wheaties. "She's expecting you on Saturday."

That bit of intelligence made me furious, but I had been putting up Miss Langley's lights since I was twelve, so I expected the call.

"It takes all day because that mean old bi—"

"Jack!" my mother said sharply. "Miss Langley is a lonely woman with no family or friends to help her. In the spirit of Christmas, I think the least we can do is put up her lights."

"We?" I said. "Then I suppose you'll be there to help me?"

I knew Mom had no intention of lending a hand. I was simply a messenger of her good will.

"Not Saturday," she said. "We're going to Evan's science fair."

My thirteen-year-old brother Evan smirked at me, practically demanding that I wipe the smile off his face with my fist. I resisted, promising myself I would get him later—without witnesses.

The Wheaties had turned into soggy sawdust and what little good cheer I possessed had evaporated.

"Maybe I'll die in a fiery bus crash by Saturday," I said. "Then I won't have to put up her damn lights."

"He said 'damn,'" my little sister Gracie said, scandalized. "Besides, I like Miss Langley. She's nice."

"You like her because you don't play softball," I said. "And also because you're nuts."

"Ho, ho, ho," my father said wearily. "Merry Christmas."
I don't think he meant it.

＊ ♣ ＊

Unfortunately, I had the bad fortune to avoid fiery buses that week and, when Saturday rolled around, I had to pay the price of my mother's belief in compulsory volunteerism. The eggnog of human kindness was not flowing in my veins and it was all I could do to drag myself to Miss Langley's house that frosty afternoon. She started in on me at once.

"You're late," she snapped.

"You get what you pay for," I mumbled.

I had never received a cent for putting up her lights, or a cup of hot chocolate, or even a cookie for wasting several hours of my valuable time.

"What?" Miss Langley said, cupping her hand to her ear. Fortunately, she was too vain to wear her hearing aid. Not that she had much to be vain about. She was a small woman, perhaps five feet tall, but she was slightly stooped, making her appear smaller. I towered over her. But what she lacked in height, she made up for in intensity. Old Lady Langley always seemed tightly coiled and ready to explode at the slightest provocation. I could feel the nervous energy radiating from her even through the storm door. That was the way she always talked to me— through the storm door. Apparently, I wasn't good enough to set foot in her house. I was just another handyman, albeit an unpaid one.

"Let's get started," I said, wondering for the hundredth time why I tolerated this nonsense. I should have been sitting in front of a roaring fire at my girlfriend's house instead of aiding and abetting Miss Scrooge. There was only one explanation: it was 1962. In those dim, dark days, even teenagers rarely told adults to cram it. It wasn't until later in the decade that we learned not to listen to anyone over thirty.

The outdoor lights were stored in two large cartons marked, originally, "Lights." I set up the ladder and began. About ten minutes into the process, Miss Langley came to the door and screamed at me. "No! No! You're doing it all wrong!"

I smiled down at her and said, "Yes, it's pretty cold."

Pretending not to understand her drove Old Lady Langley insane.

"You must make the lights even!" she screeched through the storm door.

"Yeah, it's cold all right," I said, blowing on my reddened hands and wiped my runny nose with numb fingers.

"Start again!" she commanded.

An hour later I had finished one tree to her relative satisfaction and had begun work on the second one that flanked her doorway. During that time, I had been reamed up one side and down the other, my intelligence denigrated, my manhood impugned, and my abilities as an electrician belittled. But after all the years of abuse, I had become inured to her criticism. Besides, grouchy old ladies were low on my list of priorities that Saturday. For the first time in my life, I was hopelessly, passionately in love. Her name was Diane and I found myself whispering her name to myself at odd hours and dreaming about her day and night. I actually ached inside when she wasn't near me. My love for her was extravagant, boundless, and scary. I was hooked and I couldn't understand what was happening to me.

Following the pattern that has dogged me all my life, I hadn't really fallen for Diane until she became unattainable or almost so. That summer we had hung around together, going to the movies, the beach, and a Broadway play or two. We had picnics in the park, swam in her pool, and suffered through her father's excruciatingly elaborate barbeques. We had kissed and made out in an innocent way, neither one of us expecting much nor receiving it. She laughed at my jokes, which took fortitude, and I loved the sound of her voice as she did imitations of our friends and family. I found her hilarious, but she was just a pal, not a necessary part of me. Then she moved.

If she had stayed in town, I suppose we would have seen each other and continued our casual relationship. But then she and her family absconded to the wilds of the Connecticut shore, an impossible two hours away. And once I couldn't see her every day, she became my obsession.

"It's still crooked," Miss Langley shrieked.

"Diane," I said.

"What?"

"Diane," I yelled as loud as I could.

"What?"

As I continued to string the lights, I could see her blonde hair, which flipped up in the back, her smoky blue eyes, her perfect nose, and her wide, good-humored smile—a smile I wouldn't be seeing for the next two weeks because Diane and her family were vacationing in Jamaica over the holidays. It had been a lonely fall not seeing her except on weekends and now it would be a lonely Christmas. All I had left were my dreams.

I quickly wound the final strand and plugged in both trees. The multicolored lights flared briefly, then flickered out.

"What's wrong?" Old Lady Langley snarled from behind her protective door, her breath making opaque circles on the glass.

"I don't know," I said, thinking it was my job to put on the lights, not make them work.

"Well, fix it!" she hissed.

"Sorry, got to go," I said. "I'll be back tomorrow to see if I can get them on."

Without looking back, I hightailed it home to the sound of Miss Langley's infuriated screams, bracketed by darkly muttered imprecations.

Not that things were much better at home—warmer, perhaps, but not better. My parents and younger brother were on their way to the science fair, so I had to pick up my little sister, Gracie, at a skating party some twenty miles away. Now, twenty miles is not a long distance in most of the country. Later in life, I remember driving six times that far just to have lunch in another city, but that was because I lived near an interstate. Where we were located in those days, there were no fast highways connecting a web of tiny towns. In fact, it was almost impossible to get from one hamlet to another unless you had been born and raised in the area. Directions like "turn left at the old Miller place" tended to confuse non-natives. I knew where I was going, but I also knew it would take me more than an hour to get there.

When I had first gotten my driver's license, I had sworn to my parents that I would be a conscientious chauffeur, always willing to pick up my younger siblings, always game for getting groceries. I had pictured myself leaping behind the wheel and roaring off at a moment's notice to accomplish whatever tasks had to be performed. Out of aspirin? I'm on it. Need a loaf of bread? Watch my exhaust. Evan needs a ride to soccer practice? Jump in.

That attitude lasted for about a week. Then reality set in and I found that driving was more a pain than a pleasure, more constricting than liberating. Except for a chance to be alone with Diane, driving was not the joyous celebration I had imagined it to be for half my life—especially in winter.

It was almost dark outside and beginning to snow when I trudged wearily out the door to retrieve my six-year-old sister. I didn't know it then, but I would be bringing home more than one passenger.

CHAPTER 2

My father owned an extensive and eccentric assortment of automobiles. I don't know why. He wasn't mechanically minded by any means. In fact, I don't think I ever saw him lift the hood of any car he owned. Nor was he a person who derived immense satisfaction from cleaning and polishing his vehicles. That was a job he foisted off on me and my brother. He wasn't even keen on driving great distances. Dad just enjoyed buying cars—any kind of car. They didn't have to be new. Old ones would do perfectly well. Many a time he would regale the family with the merits of an ancient junker, claiming "they don't make 'em like that anymore."

That Saturday afternoon, two relatively decent cars were in the garage for repairs and Dad had taken the Chrysler 300 to transport himself, my mother, and brother to the science fair, a trip of almost a mile. The 300 was designed to idle at 7500 rpm and could reach two hundred miles an hour going up Pike's Peak. My options for a much more rugged journey were pitiful: the midnight blue 1948 Buick Roadmaster with the grinning, big-toothed grille or the purple 1952 Dodge. That was an easy decision to make. The Buick hadn't started since the previous spring, pending some kind of major operation.

The Dodge sat forlornly in the driveway, crusted with ice and powdered with a thin layer of snow. Originally it had been black, but many seasons at the shore in summertime had pitted the chrome and blistered the paint. For a fast $39.95, however, Earl Scheib had miraculously transformed the sheet metal into a matte burgundy color. Most of the chrome had been painted burgundy, too, but what do you expect for forty bucks?

When I opened the door, I could hear the ice crack, an ominous sign because that meant no one had driven the car for several days. I knew I hadn't and I also knew my mother, who was all of five-foot-three, hated the Dodge because it was so huge. She had a difficult time seeing over the ship-size steering wheel and reaching the pedals at the same time. Worse, the car weighed about three tons and did not have power steering. Mom didn't so much drive that car as wrestle with it. Watching her attempt to parallel park the monstrous machine was a spectator sport our whole town enjoyed. She swore she would rather walk twenty miles than drive the Dodge around the corner. And she meant it.

I hunched over the wheel, half my brain working on driving calculations and half thinking about Diane. I knew I was losing the war of the long-distance romance. I could feel Diane slipping away from me. When we talked on the phone, she would tell me casual things that a normal person would probably have shrugged off. But I wasn't normal: I was in love and insanely jealous.

"I had a great time with Billy Johnson last night," she had told me last week.

"Oh, yeah?" I had tried to sound nonchalant, but I had

felt my stomach heave and my face redden. *Who the hell was Billy Johnson?*

"Yeah, we went to the movies and saw *Lawrence of Arabia*," she had said. "He was cool."

Billy or T.E. Lawrence? I wondered.

"You went on a date?" I had asked incredulously.

"Of course not," she had said. "I'm going with you. I just went with a bunch of friends, that's all."

I had failed to grasp the distinction, but I hadn't said anything, mostly because I didn't know what to say. The one thing I did know was that Diane wasn't going to wait around forever for a guy like me. As young and inexperienced as I was, I had this odd romantic notion that once you fell in love, that was it. Period. *Fini.* You couldn't ever love anyone else again. That was an unsettling notion at sixteen. Barring the expected nuclear holocaust, I had at least a half-century ahead of me.

I drove slowly over the icy streets, intent on keeping the Dodge under control. I cut through back roads and finally arrived at the amusement park that doubled as an ice-skating rink in the winter. I parked the car, spotted Gracie among a gaggle of first graders, and swooped down on her from behind. She shrieked as I lifted her high in the air and slammed her down on my shoulders. She giggled and squirmed and beat me on the head, pretending she was angry. I pretended her tiny fists were doing great damage. It was a game we played.

As a polite teenager, an oxymoron if ever there was one,

I thanked the mother of the birthday girl and congratulated the little girl herself. She blushed and said, "I wish I had a big brother to pick me up instead of my mother." Even if Diane took a dim view of me, I was a hit with the milk tooth set.

Out in the parking lot, Gracie made a valiant effort to climb Mt. Dodge, but I had to give her a leg up to the front seat as if I were boosting her into a saddle. It was a long way up for a little kid. She sank into the foam rubber bench, almost disappearing from sight. We had barely cleared the lot when the snow really began to fall. Small flakes, I knew from my weather-wizard grandmother, meant accumulation. And accumulation meant it would take us forever to get home.

I felt the car fishtail to the left and steered into it as I had been instructed by my driving-wizard father. Sure enough, we straightened out and plowed on. That was when Gracie got chatty.

"I'm getting a kitty for Christmas," she said with all the fervor of a tent show evangelist. "And she'll be pretty and white and have blue eyes."

"No, you're not," I said.

"Santa said so," she told me, as if that put an end to any argument.

In her heart, Gracie knew the score about Santa Claus, but she was so desperate for a cat that she was willing to believe some bearded fat guy from Macy's was about to come down the chimney with one. Months earlier, she had convinced herself that the Easter Bunny was going to deliver a cat to her—stuffed inside an egg. She had been sorely disappointed when every single egg had proved to be kittyless.

"It's not fair," she had wailed.

And it wasn't, but that was reality around our house. For years, my brother and I had begged and pleaded for dogs, cats, and ponies, but all we ever got was the occasional odd hamster and goldfish. The lack of animals in our lives stemmed from a twenty-year feud between my parents. Mom loved cats, but was decidedly cool toward dogs. Dad hated cats. I mean, he *really* hated them. Worse, he was allergic to their fur. A cat within ten yards of him would make his eyes water, his nose run, and his disposition sour. He might have agreed to a dog, but he was stymied by my mother's dictum that a dog, unless it had at least ten thousand acres to roam around upon, would be unhealthy and unhappy. Our house was decidedly short on land and heavy on traffic, a combination Mom thought would prove demeaning and deadly to any canine. Or so she said. Frankly, I think if we had lived in the middle of Montana, Mom would have found some other objection. Caught between the warring parties, my brother and I had battled valiantly, but like Robert E. Lee, we were on the wrong side of history. Despite her passion for a pussycat, Gracie didn't have a chance.

"You don't have a chance," I said. "Why don't you play the radio?"

"I don't know how to work it," she said.

"Turn some knobs," I suggested, for the truth was, I didn't know how to work it either. No one did. Even Marconi would have been baffled.

Picture an old-time radio, the kind that used to broadcast episodes of *Little Orphan Annie* and the speeches of FDR. Newsreels always presented an all-American family, ears cupped, leaning toward the room-size radio set, relieved to hear that all they had to fear was fear itself. Now take that radio, shove it into the dashboard of the Dodge, add a few dozen knobs and levers, and a dial that was two feet across. That was the production model for 1952.

The radio extended from windshield to floor and from the passenger side to the driver's right elbow—all that space just to receive weak AM signals. Like seat belts, FM was not highly regarded at the time.

With beginner's luck, Gracie somehow managed to get the vacuum tubes warmed up and we strained to hear the strains of "Stranger on the Shore."

"That's a poopy song," Gracie said, bestowing her highest expression of disdain on Aker Bilk and his hit.

I looked over at Gracie and smiled. She was a small child with brown hair cut in a pageboy style. My father insisted that she wear her hair short because when it was long, it always wound up in her mouth when she ate. That drove my father crazy. He was a table manners maniac and the thought of eating a hairy hamburger made him froth with indignation.

We made our way through the whirling snow, eventually turning onto a commercial street lined with businesses and fast food places. Gracie looked wistfully out the window and told me she was hungry.

"What did you eat at the rink?" I asked.

"Nothin'," she said. "Just some popcorn, a hot dog, some Jujubes, a Tootsie Roll, and—"

"Jeez."

"—and ice cream and cake."

"Poor starving kid," I said.

"What was that?" Gracie asked suddenly.

"What?"

"That noise," she said.

I listened carefully and was rewarded with one of the most sickening sounds in the world, the thump, thump, thump of a flat tire.

"Damn."

"Jack said a bad word," Gracie said with a sigh.

For all its other faults, the Dodge's biggest defect was its lack of anything resembling a real tire. My father drove the car a grand total of three miles a week and didn't see much purpose in spending good money on good rubber, especially when he owned so many other needy cars, which, like baby birds, all clamored for attention and valve jobs.

Even a casual inspection would confirm that the Dodge's four tires were worn beyond recognition. A magnifying glass might reveal latent images of the original tread, but to the naked eye, the tires were as bald as Yul

Brynner's head. When I brought this safety hazard to his attention, my father had said, "You can read a newspaper right through them." He seemed to be proud that he was setting a new endurance record, but it was a bad year for Goodyear.

Partially blinded by the swirling snow, I wrestled the wobbly car into a parking lot shared by a McDonald's and a Carvel franchise.

"Can I have some ice cream?" Gracie asked, looking at the giant cone atop the Carvel stand. Carvel was famous for its soft ice cream once found only on the boardwalk at the New Jersey shore.

"No, but how about a burger, fries, and a Coke?" I asked.

I knew nutrition. No more of that unhealthy ice cream for Gracie.

For less than seventy-five cents, I bought her a meal and watched her pick at it. The vast quantity of food she had eaten at the skating rink had apparently been enough, despite her protestations. I ate a few fries from the paper packet and wished I was sharing them with Diane.

CHAPTER 3

Out in the parking lot, I removed the spare, tire iron, and jack. The wind whipped the snow into a fury, pelting me in the face. I was much too manly in those days to wear gloves and my hands were soon red, raw, and dirty. Gracie was vainly attempting to make a snowball, but the dry snow failed to pack.

"Get in the car," I told her. Her slight weight would not make jacking up the Dodge any harder.

"I want to play on the swings," Gracie said, pointing to a snow-covered swing set at the back of the lot.

"It's too cold. You'll freeze," I said.

"No, I won't," she said petulantly.

"Suit yourself," I said.

About four minutes in the ten-degree weather would convince her quicker than I could.

I worked quickly and efficiently and was just wrenching the last frozen lug nut into place when I heard Gracie's high, tinny voice calling my name through the gloom. I looked into the blowing snow, but I couldn't see anything. I slammed the hubcap on and went searching for her.

Although she was only a few yards away, I had a difficult time finding her. She was standing by the swing, a large milkshake container gripped in her mittened hands.

"I found her. I found her!" Gracie cried excitedly.

"Found who?" I asked.

"My kitty, the one Santa promised me," she said, holding out the paper cup for me to inspect.

I looked down at the Carvel cup and saw a grayish-brown tail sticking out of it.

"It looks more like a rat to me," I said. "Just put it back where you found it and let's go. The tire's all fixed."

"It's not a rat," Gracie said, pouting. "It's my kitty."

"Then it's probably dead," I said.

"No, I heard her meow."

I looked closer at the rigid tail protruding from the cup. Whatever was in there had to be frozen to death, I thought.

"That's not a kitten, it's a frozen cat-sicle," I said. "You can pick it up by the tail and lick it."

Gracie looked up at me with teary eyes and her bottom lip began to tremble. That was a sure sign that the water-works were about to be turned on full blast.

"Bring it over to the car and let me take a look," I said, hoping to forestall a storm of tears.

In the murky glare of the Dodge's interior light, I carefully slid the creature from the cup. It was a kitten, more or less, its fur covered with blood, ice, and chocolate milk-shake. I felt its chest and found, to my surprise, a weak heartbeat.

"Is she all right?" Gracie asked anxiously.

"No, it's almost a goner," I said. "I think the best thing you can do is put it back where you found it."

"No," Gracie wailed, letting loose the tears. "She's my kitty. You've got to fix her, Jack."

My small knowledge of cats did not include an owner's manual.

"It's not a toy, Gracie. You can't just fix it."

"You fixed my doll," she said, the tears streaming down her face.

"This is different," I said. "It's a living, almost breathing, creature."

Gracie's face contorted in pain. All she could say was, "Please?"

I have to admit, I was a sucker when it came to tears. I would do almost anything to prevent Gracie from crying, including doing something irrational like letting her keep a half-dead kitten. But it was cold and I wanted to get home.

"All right," I said. "Get in the back seat and be careful. It could have rabies or distemper or the plague," I said, handing her the frigid little bundle of dirty fur, hoping the cold air would kill whatever microorganisms the cat was harboring. I was not only a nutritionist, but a budding epidemiologist as well.

"Thank you, thank you," Gracie squealed, throwing her arms around my waist.

The back seat of the Dodge was big enough to host a square dance—with room left over for a few extra bales of hay. Gracie was almost invisible back there as she cradled the kitten in her lap and spoke to it soothingly. She petted it gently with her small fingers.

"Wrap it in this," I said, handing her my scarf.

"But that's your new scarf," Gracie said.

"The cat needs it more than I do," I said. "Just keep it warm and maybe it will live until we get home."

We drove through the whirling snow at a sedate pace, which magically transformed an hour's drive into two. I expected another flat at any moment and could see myself standing by the side of the road waiting for my incensed father to rescue us.

"How's the cat doing?" I asked Gracie as we neared home.

"I can feel her breathing," Gracie said. "But she hasn't said anything."

"No kidding?" I said. "But look, Gracie, we've got a real problem. Mom and Dad aren't going to let you keep it."

"But Santa gave her to me," Gracie said, her voice trembling.

"You'll make Dad sick," I said. "He's got allergies."

"I'll keep her in my room," Gracie said. "No one will ever know."

"Well, there you go," I said. "Good plan."

"Don't laugh at me, Jack. Help me and my kitty."

Poor little Gracie had worked herself up into a frenzy over this cat nonsense and it was all my fault. I should have tossed the damn thing in the bushes and have been done with it. But trying to placate her, I had made the situation worse. The problem was, I could deny Gracie almost nothing. She had been a change-of-life baby, a complete surprise to the entire family. I was almost eleven years old when she was born, and as soon as I discovered she posed no threat to me, I loved her mightily. But I didn't really think of her as a sister. I was so much older than she was, I felt like her uncle, not her brother, and therefore I was indulgent of her whims. Brothers are not so forgiving. Ask Evan.

"I'm not laughing at you," I said. "But if you want to keep that thing, you've got to hide it from Mom and Dad."

"Where?"

"The basement, I guess. Nobody ever goes down there except you," I said.

Gracie practically lived in the "fort" I had built for her in the basement. It consisted of three large cardboard boxes and a few old blankets thrown over on a clothesline. The fort was pretty crude, but Gracie liked to hide down there when things got confusing upstairs. She had transferred her tea set, stuffed animals, and dolls to the fort and held elaborate social events in the dark. That probably meant she would be an early candidate for a lengthy course of psychiatry, but my parents, having raised two sons, weren't much worried about odd behavior in children.

"She can live in my fort with me," Gracie said happily.

"No. You have to sleep in your room or Mom will get suspicious," I said. "You can't say a word."

"I promise," she said.

The last time Gracie had tried to keep a secret, she kept it to herself for all of eight minutes before blurting it out. I wondered how long she would last with Mom grilling her about the afternoon's activities.

"We'll go in the house as if nothing happened," I told her. "Then, just go to bed. I'll get the cat and sneak it into the basement. But don't get your hopes up, the kitten probably won't make it through the night."

My thought was to get up early in the morning and toss the corpse in the trash before Gracie found it. I would tell her the kitten had been called away to cat heaven.

"She'll be all right," Gracie said. "You'll fix her, Jack. I know you will."

Her irrational faith in me was annoying because I felt myself being dragged further and further into a conspiracy I wanted no part of.

"Don't count on it," I said. "And remember—not a word."

I parked the Dodge in the driveway, helped Gracie out, and shoved the cat-sicle under the front seat. I would be back for it in a few minutes.

※ ·⋙· ※

"Where have you been?" my mother asked.

Gracie gave Mom the kid version of our adventures and, to my amazement, she didn't let on about the cat.

"It's late," my mother said when she had finished giving Gracie the third degree about the party, the skating, and the meal at McDonald's. "I want you in bed."

I winked at Gracie, who stifled a giggle and rushed off without putting up a stink about going to bed early.

The snow had just stopped when I opened the door of the Dodge and rooted around under the front seat. I found the scarf with its moribund contents. The kitten hadn't moved, but I could feel its labored breathing. The best I could do for it was to keep it as warm as possible.

I smuggled the contraband into the basement and pushed aside the blankets that served as the entry to Gracie's fort. Inside, it looked as if a tornado had swept through the basement: dolls and doll clothes were strewn about haphazardly; stuffed animals haunted the recesses; toys, books, crayons, and paints littered the floor. I put the kitten down and rewrapped it in the scarf, leaving only its nose sticking out. The concrete floor was cold, so I put the scarf-wrapped kitten in Gracie's toy baby carriage to get it off the ground. It looked ridiculous lying there like one of her discarded playthings, but it was as comfortable as I could make it for the moment. However, I thought I should get it some milk on the off chance it lived until morning.

Upstairs in the kitchen, I grabbed a glass of milk, a saucer, and for good measure, I pilfered two cans of Piels beer. My father would never miss them. The only reason he choked down a couple of them a month was because he liked the Burt and Harry Piel commercials as performed by Bob and Ray. I left the saucer full of milk right by the kitten's nose and gently petted the sleeping form.

Later, I looked in on Gracie, who was asleep. Then I retreated to my room for a well-deserved twenty minutes of mooning over Diane—and a couple of brews. But the more I tried to focus on life, love, and Diane, the more I began thinking about the little cat in the basement and its struggle to live. For its own sake, I hoped it would expire quickly and painlessly. But maybe I shouldn't just throw it out, I thought. A funeral would be more appropriate for Gracie, who, like all children, enjoyed ritual and ceremony. I would decide in the morning. So many things to decide, so few options.

The two cans of beer knocked me right out, but I still didn't sleep very well that night.

CHAPTER 4

The next morning I was up well before the sun and headed straight for the basement. I still hadn't made up my mind about holding a funeral, but I was quite sure the cat was dead.

The basement of our house was a dark and dismal place, lit only by a few low-wattage bulbs. My mother went down there once a week to do emergency laundry; Dad, in a fury, would change the occasional fuse; Evan and I avoided the place as much as possible. Other than Gracie's fort, there was not much in the basement to attract anyone. The walls and floors were cement, painted gray. Three small windows let in a few rays of sunshine in summer, but didn't alleviate the gloom of winter. A washer, a dryer, a sink, a massive asbestos-wrapped boiler, a broken gas stove, and a jumble of worn-out furniture completed the depressing picture. I had friends who had basements with pool tables, bars, TV sets, and dart boards. They called the place where their ping-pong tables resided a rec room. We had a wreck room.

The kitten was lying where I had left it; the bowl of milk was untouched. At first, I thought it had expired, but as I bent down to look at it, one amber eye opened and stared at me.

"You gotta be the toughest cat in the world," I said.

"Mew," the cat said.

I unwrapped the tiny form and inspected the damage. The kitten's fur was matted and filthy, covered with mud, blood, feces, and chocolate milkshake. Worse, I could see burn and bite marks all over its body. When it tried to move, its twisted front leg got in the way, and the kitten slumped back into the folds of the befouled scarf. It looked at me reproachfully with its one good eye.

I was still wondering what to do when I heard Gracie clumping down the rickety wooden stairs that led to the basement. Quickly, I wrapped the kitten back up, hiding the worst of its wounds.

"Is she fixed yet?" Gracie asked, poking her head inside the fort.

"Well, it's still alive," I said. "Barely."

"I knew it, Jack. I knew you could fix her," Gracie said.

"Yeah, I'm a regular Ben Casey," I said. "But I'm surprised it's not dead."

"Santa wouldn't give me a dead kitty," Gracie said, as if I were one of the dim bulbs in the basement.

I scratched the back of my head, wondering just how the hell I had gotten involved in this parlous adventure. The kitten was probably in great pain and we were torturing it by keeping it alive. If it hadn't been Sunday, I would have taken the kitten to a veterinarian to have it put down. That was the sane and humane thing to do. I made up my mind that first thing Monday, I'd take care if it. Poor Gracie would dissolve into weeping and wailing and gnashing of teeth, but it had to be done.

"Has she eaten her breakfast?" Gracie asked, noticing the saucer of milk.

"No, it won't eat," I said. "And how do you know it's a girl cat, anyway?"

"Santa told me," she said.

I had purposefully not assigned a sex to the kitten because I wanted to stay as uninvolved as possible. It was going to die and I didn't want to mourn for it.

"The Santa at Macy's?" I asked.

My mother and Gracie made an annual trip to New York City to look at the department store windows and unload a lengthy wish list on the red-suited fat man.

"No, Mommy told me he's just one of Santa's helpers," Gracie said.

"Then which Santa?"

"The *real* Santa, of course."

"And where did you run into the *real* Santa?" I asked.

"In my room," Gracie said. "I was sleeping and then I woke up and Santa told me I was going to get a girl kitty as a present."

"You were dreaming," I said.

"If I was just dreaming...how come I got a kitty?" Gracie asked.

Checkmate.

A child's world is an offbeat mixture of fantasy and reality, interchangeable states of mind that are not mutually exclusive. If Gracie believed she had been visited by the Jolly Old Elf, she really believed it, as much as she believed in the reality of the kitten before her. Her behavior in an adult would have called for institutionalization, but because she was only six everyone believed she would grow out of it. However, it is difficult for a rational person to reason with a child because children think on a different, alien level.

As a perfectly sane teenager most of the time, my only response to Gracie's tale was simple and direct: "Yeah, right."

Sarcasm, of course, is lost on children, so Gracie took it that I believed her tale of Clausian astral projection.

"She doesn't smell too good," Gracie said. "She needs a bath."

"I don't think cats take baths," I said.

"A shower?"

"They're supposed to be self-cleaning, like Mom's oven," I said.

"Mommy says that doesn't work so good," Gracie said. "Should I get the Easy Off?"

"That would do a great job," I said, picturing a bald, scalded kitten. "No, get a damp rag and I'll clean her up a bit."

Gracie returned from the sink with a dish towel soaked in water. I wrung it out and ran it over the grubby kitten. After a few swipes, an amazing thing happened. Beneath the grime and blood and milkshake was actual fur—not a dingy brown fur, but bright orange-striped fur.

"Oooh," Gracie said. "She's beautiful."

"You've got yourself a marmalade cat," I said.

"She must be a very rare breed," Gracie said.

"Yeah, a *Pussycatus americanus*," I said.

I hadn't watched all those Road Runner cartoons for nothing. If the coyote could be *Caninus hungrious* and the Road Runner could be *Birdipus speedius*, there was no reason the kitten couldn't enjoy an exalted title in the animal kingdom, too.

Nutritionist, epidemiologist, taxonomist—was there no end to my talents? Gracie was impressed.

"I knew she was special," she said.

"Yeah," I said. "The coveted *Alleycatus ordinarii*."

I finished wiping the kitten off and she looked much better, but the removal of several layers of built up filth made her wounds all the more horrendous. I could see a clear set of teeth marks that encircled her middle and she was covered with burns, some healed, some open and oozing blood and pus. One eye was crusted over, but a vigorous scrubbing got rid of the milkshake that had glued it shut.

"She can see!" Gracie squealed, as if I had preformed a miracle.

"Hallelujah!" I said in my best Elmer Gantry imitation.

"You cured her!" Gracie said, hugging me.

Suddenly, I really felt like Elmer Gantry, a fraud of particularly nasty kind. I took the remains of my scarf from the baby carriage because it was now dirtier than the kitten; then I found a red wool doll blanket to wrap her in.

"What comes after bath time?" I asked Gracie.

"Bedtime?"

"Good guess, " I said. "But let's see if we can get her to eat first. I don't think cats need any instructions when it comes to sleeping. They're famous for it."

"Why didn't she drink her milk?" Gracie asked.

"I don't know, but she's probably dehydrated."

"What's that?"

"Lacking water," I said.

Hey, I had taken tenth-grade biology and I knew about these things. I could also saw a frog in half, but that was a skill which proved to be useless in this situation, so I had to fall back on a more esoteric field of science, the aforementioned cartoonology.

I couldn't pinpoint the exact cartoon, but in several I had seen, baby animals had been fed with a red rubber glove. All you had to do was fill the glove with milk, poke a hole in one finger, and—*ta-da*!—a makeshift bottle with ersatz nipple. It worked well in cartoons and I had no reason to believe it wouldn't work in real life. The same red rubber glove, by the way, could also be used by a rabbit to imitate a rooster. The rabbit would wear the glove on his head to simulate a cockscomb and place a toilet plunger on his butt, transforming his cotton tail into tail feathers. The entire barnyard was always fooled—at least for a while.

"Go upstairs and get one of Mom's rubber gloves," I said to Gracie. "A new one, if possible. And a bottle of milk."

Mom always wore rubber gloves when she washed the dishes, which was about twice a year. She had me, Evan, and Gracie to do the dirty work as well as a perfectly good GE dishwasher. The gloves were strictly ornamental, a symbol of her housewifeliness, and she wouldn't miss one until June, if then.

Gracie brought an unopened package of Playtex Living Gloves. They were yellow, not red, which was unsettling, but I figured the principle was the same. I used my penknife to bore a hole in the index finger; then I filled the glove with a small amount of Borden's milk from the bottle Gracie had swiped from the refrigerator.

"Well, here goes," I said, squirting a test amount through the finger.

A thin stream of liquid shot into the air.

"It works!" Gracie said, amazed. "You're so smart."

"When it comes to cartoon technology, maybe," I said.

I pressed the yellow glove to the cat's mouth and squeezed. The milk spurted out all over her face. Nothing happened for a minute, then a tiny pink tongue darted from her mouth and she licked up the mess. I let her finish; then bought her a second round. In five minutes, she was sucking directly from the Playtex Living finger, proving to me that she was not only strong, but smart.

"When she's done, clean her face and wrap her in the doll blanket," I said, handing the glove to Gracie. "Then get your tail back upstairs before Mom comes looking for you."

"Where are you going?" she asked.

"To Old Lady Langley's to see if I can get her lights working," I said.

"Can I come?"

"No, after breakfast tell Mom you want to play in the fort. That way you can keep an eye on the cat. Have a tea party or something, but don't invite the kitten. She needs to sleep."

As I left, I heard Gracie croon her current favorite nursery rhyme: "Pussycat, pussycat, where have you been? I've been to London to see the queen."

Unfortunately, she didn't pronounce *been* as *bean*, so the couplet didn't rhyme.

After I dressed and went back downstairs to grab a bite to eat, I found Mom and Gracie sitting at the kitchen table talking about something. I hoped it wasn't feline related.

"Did you get Miss Langley's lights up yesterday?" she asked.

"Uh."

"Was it difficult?"

"Uh."

"Well, you are doing a nice thing for a poor old lady," she said.

That one didn't even merit an "uh."

"Didn't work. Gotta go back," I said.

I didn't like to waste subjects and pronouns on my parents. None of those flowery adjectives and adverbs for me, either. Stripped-down language, I thought, gave my speech a certain masculine quality—like that of Tarzan or Tonto. My everyday laconic grunts, too, reminded me of John Wayne or Robert Mitchum when they were being particularly ornery.

I shoved a piece of toast in my mouth and fled the possibility of an actual adult conversation.

* ☙ *

Old Lady Langley must have been up all night waiting for my return because she started yelling at me before I got anywhere near her door. I could see her gesticulating wildly from the windows of her kitchen—the same windows I used to break with regularity. Not only did Miss Langley have the misfortune of living on the left field line, she had made things worse by installing a twenty-foot span of small glass panes—many, many rows of them. I suppose a seamless plate glass window would have been more expensive to replace, but she also could have had a couple of regular windows installed instead. A well-placed ice ball would be satisfying, I thought—in a nostalgic way, of course.

"Where have you been?" Old Lady Langley screeched at me when I had worked my way around her house to the front door.

"'To London, to see the queen,'" I muttered, noting that she was without her hearing aid.

"What were you doing in Queens when you should have been fixing my lights?" she said through the storm door.

"Uh," I said, my normal self again.

From a treacherous perch on the aluminum ladder, I checked the bulbs for the telltale rattling of broken filaments, but they all seemed intact. Then I followed the heavy-duty outdoor wire to the plug by the side of her house. I unplugged the lights and plugged them back in. Nothing happened. Repeating that procedure, I was rewarded with…more nothing.

"Why are you so slow?" Miss Langley demanded. She had been watching my every move.

"Where's your fuse box?" I asked loudly and clearly.

"In the basement," she said.

"I ought to have a look at it."

"Use the bulkhead doors over there," she said, pointing to a set of wooden doors that butted against her house. They were padlocked and chained between the handles. As I was wondering what to do, a set of keys landed by my feet. She may have been old, but Miss Langley still had a pretty good arm.

The wooden doors were heavy, no doubt weighed down by a hundred years of flaking paint. They gave an eerie groan of protest when I ripped them from their resting place. A couple thousand spiders ran for their lives. No one had been down here since my favorite president, Rutherford B. Hayes, had been in office, I thought, and that was almost a century ago.

Brushing the cobwebs from my face, I walked down the brick steps and into the stygian darkness, realizing immediately that I had finally found a basement that was worse than ours. It smelled of mice, mildew, and mold. Cardboard boxes were stacked with less than military precision against the damp stone walls. Shrouded in dusty sheets was an array of discarded furniture. Or, at least, I hoped it was furniture and not something worse—like the bodies of her victims. Suddenly, two small bulbs above my head came to life and I could see Miss Langley standing at the top of the inside stairs.

"In the corner! In the corner! Over there!" Old Lady Langley yelled, pointing wildly as if she had just seen a ghost materialize out of thin air.

I found the gray metal fuse box behind a dressmaker's dummy. The dummy had no head, but its shoulders sported a wide-brimmed black hat, festooned with rhinestones and ostrich feathers. Rutherford B. Hayes would have approved, I think. Against the wall was a line of metal cylinders that were labeled *Danger! Oxygen.* Next to the dummy was a cracked brown leather bag with a red cross in a white circle emblazoned on the side. Dr. Langley, I presume? I was going to open it to see what was inside, but Miss Langley screamed at me to hurry up.

Reasoning that the outside fuse would be the last of the eight, I unscrewed that one. The lights in the basement suddenly went out. So much for reasoning. I tried one after another until I found the one with the broken metal band showing through the glass viewing port and replaced it with a spare lying on top of the box.

"That should do it," I yelled up the stairs.

The lights in the basement went out again, but this time it was Miss Langley who had flicked the switch. No sense in paying for electricity when it was only the less-than-handy boy in the basement, I suppose.

I made my way up the stairs and plugged the lights in again. This time they blazed forth with color, brightening the gray morning with sparking red, white, blue, and green. The trees looked damn good, I thought, locking the basement doors and returning the keys to Miss Langley.

"Leave them on the steps," she said from behind the storm door.

"*Merry* effin' *Christmas!*" I shouted, making sure she could hear only two of the three words. Then I flipped the keys on the steps and left her to enjoy her wicked witchery or whatever it was she did in her spare time when she wasn't bothering me.

❋ 💣 ❋

I found Gracie hidden away in her fort, having a tea party with her stuffed animals and dolls. I crawled inside and looked at the kitten in the dim light. She was sleeping.

"What should I call her?" Gracie asked me.

"How about Dirty, Filthy, or Hungry?" I said. "Sneezy, Dopey, or Doc?"

"Nooo," she said, horrified. "I could call her Fluffy."

"This cat is many things," I said, "but fluffy it ain't."

"Kitty?"

"Hackneyed," I said, using a vocabulary word I had learned in school.

"Does that mean you don't like it?" she asked me.

"Yes," I said. "Think of something original."

She squinted her eyes and stared at the sleeping kitten. I could hear the small wheels grinding in her small brain.

"Orangey," she said triumphantly.

"Descriptive, but not interesting," I said.

"Stripey?"

"Yuck."

"I know, I'll call her Carvel just like where we found her."

"Well, that's better than Cuppy," I said. "I guess it will do."

CHAPTER 5

D r. August H.E. Lindemann was the only veterinarian I knew. I didn't really know him, but my parents did, and everybody in town had heard of him. A tall, blond man with a penchant for double-breasted pinstripe suits, he had a monopoly on the local small animal practice. Anyone who was socially conscious, and in 1962 being socially conscious meant caring about one's place in society, availed themselves of his services. It was important back then to attend the right church, wear the right clothes, vacation in the right spots, eat at the right restaurants, and receive the right treatments from the right physicians. Therefore, it would not have been right at all to take Fido to a cut-rate vet when the glittering Dr. August H.E. Lindemann was available. Assuming, of course, Fido was the right sort of dog.

Dr. Lindemann's animal hospital was located in a nearby town and housed in a creepy Victorian mansion smack in the middle of a residential neighborhood. A discreet metal sign informed Gracie and me that we were, indeed, in the proximity of the great man himself.

I parked the Dodge down the street and we crunched through the snow to the Addams-esque house. Inside, the waiting room looked unchanged from a hundred years ago. Horsehair sofas, intricately carved tables, painted porcelain lamps, and uncomfortable little chairs complete with lace doilies sat amid giant potted palms and rubber trees. The floor was covered with a red-and-blue Oriental rug that had seen better days. At a time when Swedish Modern had swept the country, Dr. Lindemann's office was a retrograde curiosity. Queen Victoria would have been at home here.

"It looks just like inside Miss Langley's house," Gracie said.

"You've been in Miss Langley's house?" I asked her.

"Sure."

I wondered if she were joking. I had never been allowed inside, except in the spooky basement, and I was the one who set up her damn Christmas lights every year. Gracie obviously moved in social circles denied to me. In fact, she knew almost everyone within walking distance of our house. I was far more discriminating.

We stood in the foyer, taking in the red velvet wallpaper and looking at the people sitting on the uncomfortable chairs. I spotted two golden retrievers, a Lab, a yappy poodle, and some kind of dog that had no hair. There was also a Macaw in a cage and several snobbish Siamese cats.

"I came to get my cat fixed," Gracie said, thrusting the blanket-wrapped kitten under the nose of a middle-aged woman sitting at an ornate desk.

"Do you have an appointment?" she asked, leaning away from the filthy kitten.

Gracie looked up at me.

"It's not a good idea to say 'fixed' in a veterinarian's office," I said. "But, no, we were hoping Dr. Lindemann might take a moment to look at this stray. She's in pretty bad shape. In pain, probably."

"Make an appointment," she said. "We're booked through February."

"On March first, this cat will be long dead," I said. "This is an emergency."

"Try the animal hospital in White Plains. They'll take anyone," the woman said.

I guess Gracie and I were the great unwashed "anyone."

"Look, my parents know Dr. Lindemann and I go to school with his kids," I said, on the theory that it is not what you know, but who you know.

That changed her attitude.

"We could squeeze you in on February tenth," she said, as if she were doing me a favor.

I had tried sincerity and name-dropping, but neither had moved this Cerberus guarding the entrance to Dr. Lindemann's lair. What, I wondered, were we going to do now? Then we were rescued by one of Gracie's four million friends.

A stout lady in a tartan wrap and a matching tam strolled through the waiting room, leading a shiny red Irish setter. She spotted us and *yoo-hoo*ed at Gracie.

"Hi, Mrs. Thompson. Hi, Paddy. Good boy." Gracie said, petting the dog with one hand and keeping a death grip on the kitten with the other.

"Where did you get the kitty?" Mrs. Thompson asked. She had to restrain her dog, who was eyeing Carvel as if she would make a tasty hors d'oeuvre.

"Santa gave her to me, but she's sick and Jack said we had to take her to the veteran and get her fixed so she can live with me in my fort," Gracie said in a rush. "At Carvel's."

"Oh," Mrs. Thompson said, trying to make sense of Gracie's ramblings.

"But this lady won't let us in because we don't have a 'pointment and my kitty is going to die if she isn't fixed, which is what Jack said," Gracie continued, starting to cry.

"Poor thing," Mrs. Thompson said.

Whether she was referring to the kitten or Gracie, I wasn't sure.

"Oh, for heaven's sake, Laura," Mrs. Thompson said to the woman behind the desk. "Let the child take her kitten in. She can have my appointment. We can do Paddy's physical next week or next month or next year."

It must have hurt her to turn away a regular customer, but a grudging Laura agreed. I took Mrs. Thompson aside and thanked her profusely, telling her she had perhaps saved the life of a kitten.

"I don't like cats," Mrs. Thompson said. "But I do like Gracie and I'm not overly fond of that pompous idiot Laura. Heel, Paddy, time to go home."

Gracie and I sat on a hard couch and waited our turn. I asked my little sister where she had met our savior.

"I play with Paddy sometimes," she said. "He likes to catch tennis balls in his mouth, but he won't give them back unless he gets a cookie."

Gracie always amazed me with her encyclopedic knowledge of our neighbors—human, feline, and canine. She had begun her peregrinations at the age of two, sneaking out of the house at odd hours, knocking on random doors and demanding cookies. My mother had tried everything to stop her wanderings, but by the time Gracie was three, she was an institution. It was an embarrassing and time-consuming process to accompany her anywhere. She would spend hours, it seemed, saying hello to people on the street, inquiring about their children, their parents, their pets, and their flower gardens. I would hover nervously, inanely nodding my head, and wondering just who the hell all these people were. Gracie loved them all. I wasn't too keen on anyone, except Diane.

A nurse in a white uniform finally ushered us into the inner sanctum, a place so exclusive that you needed to make reservations months in advance. I put the kitten on the table in the center of the small examination room and looked around. The white walls were covered with degrees and certificates proclaiming Dr. August H.E. Lindemann a bona fide doctor of veterinary medicine. But other than a table, a white chair, a sink, and a stainless steel cabinet, the room was bare. I wasn't impressed. At least when you made reservations at the Waldorf-Astoria Hotel, you got a little class—or so my father said.

The nurse returned with the doctor in tow. He was enormously tall and painfully thin. Dr. Lindemann towered over me and I was almost six feet tall at the time. His blond hair was combed straight back, leaving a widow's peak that pointed like an arrow toward his aquiline nose and square jaw. True to form, he was wearing pinstripe suit pants and a white lab coat. His black wingtips were shone to perfection.

I introduced Gracie and myself, stressing that we had met on previous occasions. I don't think he remembered me, but he was polite.

"We found this abandoned kitten," I told him. "Gracie here insisted on bringing it home. Could you look at it?"

"Her name is Carvel," Gracie said, as if that might be helpful in the diagnosis.

Dr. Lindemann stared at the tiny creature with a mixture of pity and disbelief on his chiseled face. I suppose he spent his days looking at pampered pets that needed to lose weight and didn't have many strays as patients. He reached down and gently touched the kitten as if he wanted to confirm that such a scruffy creature had actually invaded his examination room. This was no sleek Persian or sassy Siamese, but a desperately ill and abused animal. His long fingers traced along the kitten's backbone and I noticed that his hand was bigger than Carvel's whole body. That almost made me laugh. Here was a dignified and distinguished man, serious and professional down to his wingtips and stethoscope, seriously and professionally examining a damaged piece of fluff like Carvel. I couldn't help thinking that such an important-looking veterinarian should have been doing something more important—like curing cancer or preventing heart attacks.

Dr. Lindemann pulled a thermometer from the pocket of his lab coat and shook it. Then he inserted it into the cat's rectum. That got her attention. She raised her head from the table and meowed. Anyone would.

"Low," he said, and the nurse wrote the number down on a clipboard she had cradled in her arm. Then he put his stethoscope to his ears and listened to Carvel's heart and lungs.

"Upper respiratory infection. Fluid in the lungs," he said, hooking the stethoscope around his neck and palpating the kitten's stomach.

"No unusual enlargements or obstructions," Dr. Lindemann intoned.

"What's 'structions?" Gracie whispered to me.

"Obstructions," I said. "Blockages."

"What's blockages?"

"This could go on forever," I said. "I'll tell you later if you're still interested."

Dr. Lindemann poked a light into the kitten's ears and looked around.

"Brownish material obstructing the ear canal," he said. "I've never seen anything like it."

"Mites?" asked the nurse.

"No."

"It could be milkshake," I said, realizing my cleanup job had been less than thorough. I told him how we had found the cat.

Dr. Lindemann looked appalled, but he sniffed Carvel's ear.

"Milkshake. Chocolate. In the ear canal," he said for the nurse, who wrote it down. "Milkshake," he repeated, as if he had discovered the cat had leprosy or syphilis or some equally unlikely malady. "If she drank some, it probably kept her alive when she was out in the cold."

The nurse scurried around the room and handed Dr. Lindemann a cotton swab on a stick. He dipped it in alcohol and cleaned Carvel's ears with a lot more finesse than I could have ever mustered. Then he took the kitten's head in his enormous hands and peered deeply into Carvel's green-gold eyes. Carvel stared right back at him, daring him to do something to her.

"Conjunctivitis. Redness of upper and lower membranes. Yellowish discharge. Milkshake in the left eye," he said clinically, or as clinically as he could under the ridiculous circumstances.

"Pale membranes in the mouth, indicating anemia. Possible internal parasites," he said. "Now, let's look at that leg."

When he touched her left foreleg, Carvel whimpered. I didn't know cats could whimper, but this one did. She was in pain.

"What's wrong?" Gracie asked.

"She's got a broken leg," Dr. Lindemann said.

"Like we got a flat tire," I explained. "Except that Carvel's got no spare."

"She's got three spare feets," Gracie informed me.

Dr. Lindemann wrapped the kitten's leg in cotton; then

he produced a metal splint and wrapped everything together with white adhesive tape. The result was like the plaster cast I had worn when I had broken my arm the summer I was twelve, but much softer.

"It's fortunate that the break is in the lower part of the leg," Dr. Lindemann said. "If the femur or the humerus had been broken, she would need surgery and a splint wouldn't do much good."

"What's humerus?" Gracie asked.

"Must be the funny bone," I said.

There were limits to my grasp of tenth-grade biology. I only got a *B*.

Dr. Lindemann shot me a look of disapproval, but he continued, "She may have a permanent limp after the leg heals. However, she will still be able to get around."

"That reminds me," I said to the veterinarian. "Is it a girl, I mean, a female cat?"

Cats are not notorious for flaunting their reproductive equipment and I was curious to see if Gracie's prediction was correct.

"Yes," Dr. Lindemann said, acknowledging my ignorance.

"Told you," Gracie said. "Santa said so."

"I'm going to give her a shot of penicillin to counteract the respiratory infection," he said.

The nurse handed him a large needle and Gracie turned a lovely shade of chartreuse.

"Don't look," I said, spinning her around by the shoulders and pointing her away from the table. "And no barfing."

I could feel Gracie trembling under my hands. She was whimpering worse than the cat had been. She had always had a severe aversion to needles. According to my mother, one look at a needle caused Gracie to a) throw up, b) faint, c) pitch a fit, d) all of the above. Getting shots never bothered me much since I was twelve—the pain was a whole lot less than falling out of a cherry tree and breaking an arm.

When he was done, Dr. Lindemann told us he was going to give Carvel subcutaneous fluids. I knew subcutaneous meant under the skin, but I wasn't prepared for the yard-long needle he brandished like a sword. At first, I thought it was a movie prop. It looked perfect for a Three Stooges short in which the mad scientist chases Curly, Larry, and Moe around the secret laboratory, trying to stick them. I could feel it plunging through my body and reevaluated my dismissal of needles in general. Carvel, too, must have sensed what was coming because she let out a weak meow of protest.

"Holy sh—"

"Jack!" Gracie reprimanded me, her back still to the table.

"This will work relatively quickly to restore her fluids," Dr. Lindemann said.

I guess, I thought, wondering if I should turn around like Gracie and miss this particular therapy.

The giant barrel of the needle glinted ominously in the pale sunlight streaming through the window. The nurse hooked up the Texas-size needle to a clear plastic bag filled with fluids and handed it to the doctor.

With a demented gleam in his eye, Captain-Doctor Ahab Lindemann drove his harpoon deep into the orange-striped whalette. Well, not quite, but he inserted the needle into the kitten's back, right between the shoulder blades. I thought of my mother skewering the Thanksgiving turkey to keep the stuffing in and I winced.

Gracie chose that moment to turn around and see what was going on. Her light-green color suddenly vanished and her face took on a corpse-like pallor. Her eyes rolled up in her head and she fluttered gracefully to the floor like a dying ballerina.

I bent down and picked her up. She was totally inert.

"Take her to the waiting room," the nurse said, as the vet continued to pump fluids into the stunned kitten. "She'll be all right. It happens sometimes. Just last week a college girl from Scarsdale collapsed right here on this table."

I guess that meant we were in good company. If it could happen to a college girl from Scarsdale, we had nothing to be embarrassed about.

I dragged a limp and unresponsive Gracie to the Victorian waiting room, hoping I hadn't killed her. That would have been a tough one to explain to my parents.

I put Gracie down on a purple paisley sofa and raised her feet, presumably to send the blood back to her head from wherever it had been when she got a gander at the king-size needle. In a few minutes, her eyelids flickered and she rejoined the living.

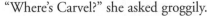

"Where's Carvel?" she asked groggily.

"She's fine," I said, not really knowing. "How are you?"

"I don't know. What happened?" she asked, struggling to sit up.

"You fainted when you saw that big needle," I said. "I told you not to look."

"I'm thirsty," she said, pushing herself upright on the couch. "Is everybody looking at us?"

"Naw," I said. "Apparently, it's kind of a tradition in Scarsdale. They do it all the time."

I brought her a paper cup of water from the cooler in the corner and she knocked it off in a single gulp, spilling less than a quarter of it on her sweater.

Suddenly, the air of sedate expectation in the room evaporated and was replaced by a nervous excitement, the kind of rustling and buzzing that might happen when royalty or movie stars made an appearance. I saw Dr. Lindemann making his way toward us. The dozen women in attendance all sat up straight in their uncomfortable chairs and patted their hair to make sure it was still there, I guess. Several of them reached for their compacts to check their makeup. With a polished and naturally aristocratic way, Dr. Lindemann worked the crowd. He bowed to some of the ladies, smiled at others, and said a couple of words to a favored few. The ladies preened and practically giggled. No wonder this guy was successful, I thought, wishing I had his obvious power over women, even if the women in question were all ancient. Depressingly, the average age of the women in the room was probably a decrepit thirty years old or so.

"How are you feeling, little girl?" the good doctor asked Gracie.

"OK," she said, an adoring smile on her face. "Even if you had to shoot her with a needle, Jack says you are the best veteran in the state and I'm glad you fixed my kitty."

Of course, I had said no such thing, but poor little Gracie was doing her best to butter him up. I would have thought that feminine wiles were wasted on Dr. Lindemann, but when Gracie crawled off the couch and flung herself into his arms, he allowed her to plant several sloppy kisses on his cheek. The women in the room looked jealous.

Dr. Lindemann was as gentle with Gracie as he had been with the kitten and he placed her back on the couch

"Jack, may I see you in my office?" he said.

Gracie started to get up, but Dr. Lindemann told her to stay where she was and rest. She didn't put up any resistance. Like the rest of the females in the room, she was totally under his spell.

I followed him down a brown carpeted hallway to his consulting office, which was clad in well-oiled oak paneling and dominated by a desk capable of handling carrier aircraft. I recognized a Cezanne and a Utrillo in places of honor on his wall and could only assume they were originals. There must have been good bucks in treating cat coughs and dog digestion, I decided.

He sat in a massive leather chair and said, "I didn't want to tell you this in front of your sister, but you have a very sick and very abused kitten."

I knew that, so I said, "I know that."

"It's going to cost a lot of money to attempt to save her," he said. "And there are no guarantees."

"Do you want to put her down?" I asked.

"I never want to do that," he said. "But you have to be realistic. For a dollar contribution, you can rescue a kitten from a shelter. And that kitten would be healthy and have all its shots."

"Look, Dr. Lindemann, when I came here I wanted the cat put out of its misery, but I've changed my mind. She's the toughest kitten I've ever seen. She's got guts. By all rights she should be dead by now. Why push her into an early grave?"

An Early Grave was the title of a mystery I was reading. It was a terrible book, but I admired the title and used it every chance I got.

"Besides, how much can it cost?" I asked. "Suppose I had a hundred bucks, would that be enough?" A hundred dollars was as much money as I could conceive of then, and it was about as attainable as a cool million.

"Probably not," he said. "And remember, I can't promise you she'll live more than a few days."

"Okay," I said with an exaggerated sigh. "You can put her down on one condition."

"What's that?"

"You have to adopt Gracie," I said. "I don't want to be around my sister if you kill her cat. She thinks Santa Claus meant for her to have it. To her, the kitten is a mystical gift. If Carvel dies on her own, I can tell her some kind of bull that will suffice. But she'll blame me for making her take the kitten to you in the first place. She'll cry and carry on until she's twenty-one. I'm a coward, Dr. Lindemann, and I can't stand fifteen years of crying. So you'll have to adopt Gracie and take her off my hands."

Dr. Lindemann didn't quite know if I was kidding or not, so he retreated to a reflective pose, one, I presume, that had worked well for him with his usual clients. Of course, he wasn't used to dealing with Mad Boy and Fainting Sister, a pair of less-than-super heroes.

"Well, if you feel that strongly about it, I'll do my best to treat her. I'll have to keep her here for a few days, but I warn you, it will be expensive," he said. "I'll send the bill to your parents."

"We have a slight problem. My parents don't know about the cat and if they did, they would make us get rid of it. You won't tell them, will you?"

"No, but it is a difficult task to hide a cat, isn't it?"

"Not so far," I said. "We'll tell my parents eventually, but right now I think it's best they don't know. Think about those fifteen years of endless crying."

"Well, I'll tell you what," he said, smiling for the first time. His teeth were perfect, naturally. "I'll give you penicillin for the respiratory infection. Watch her closely because it might turn into pneumonia. I'll also give you some salve for her burns. Keep her warm and make sure she drinks plenty of fluids."

"What should we feed her?" I asked.

He named a brand of cat food, but said she would probably live on liquids alone for the next few days, if she lived at all.

"Thanks, Dr. Lindemann," I said, really meaning it.

"And keep the cast on her leg for a month. Then bring her back, I'll remove it, and see how she's progressing," he said.

"Thanks," I said again. "What do I owe you?"

"Nothing," he said. "Speaking in my official capacity as the greatest 'veteran' in the state, I'd say that a present from Santa Claus is free."

Chapter 6

Gracie and I lumbered through traffic in the Dodge until we came to a supermarket. There we purchased cat food, litter, and other products designed to make each of the kitten's eight remaining lives more luxurious than the next. At Gracie's insistence, I also plunked down nine-five cents for a rubber mouse that squeaked in an unconvincing way.

"She likes toys," Gracie told me, although how she had come by that piece of intelligence escaped me.

The kitten, wrapped in her blanket, dozed fitfully until we arrived back at the house. I went inside to gather intelligence on troop movements and found to my relief that the place was deserted. We skulked about gathering up the tools we would need and retreated to Gracie's fort.

When I unwrapped Carvel, I was shocked once again by her appearance. The subcutaneous infusion had given her a noticeable hump back and, with her coloring, she looked like a tiny camel.

"Maybe we can get her a job as an extra in *Lawrence of Arabia*," I said.

"What?" Gracie asked, absorbed in looking at her poor, bedraggled pussycat.

"Or we could call her Quasimodo," I continued, planning an acting career for the kitten. Animal actors made millions, I knew. Lassie, for example, could buy and sell my family a thousand times over and all he had to do was rescue Uncle Petrie from a hole every week. Carvel needed a job. How else was I going to get back the $14.95 I had spent on feline supplies?

Gracie, as usual, had no idea what I was talking about and got right to the point.

"Fix her, Jack," she said.

Thoughts of a Hollywood career evaporated when I checked out the kitten's burns and sores. I applied the ointment the vet had given me and told Gracie that we had to put it on morning and night and to try to keep Carvel from licking it off. Too sick to protest, the little camel lay there unprotesting as I daubed her with the foul-smelling medicine. She would have to be pretty hungry to want to eat that gunk, I thought.

Gracie stood up, looked down on the scene, and announced that if she connected the sores with a magic marker, she would make a picture of the United States with the kitten's bandaged front leg serving as Florida. However patriotic her intent, I dissuaded her from trying.

"Let's see if we can get her to swallow this penicillin," I said.

"I hate pills," Gracie said, wrinkling her nose. "They make me throw up."

"Well, I hope Carvel is braver than you," I said.

I had no way of knowing it then, but attempting to get a cat to take a pill called for more courage than good sense. But, filled with hope, I cradled Carvel in my arm, opened her mouth with my thumb and forefinger, ignored a menacing row of needle-like teeth, and calmly tried to place the pill on her pink tongue. She slammed her jaw shut, impaling my forefinger with at least four of her six sharp teeth.

"Dammit!" I shouted, leaping to my feet. The kitten held onto my finger like a pit bull as I waved her around in the air trying to get her to release me. She wasn't budging.

"Don't hurt her, Jack," Gracie wailed.

"Hurt her? She's hurting me," I gasped, finally prying her off my finger and putting her on the floor.

"Now I'll probably get rabies," I moaned, clutching my bleeding finger.

"What's that?" Gracie asked.

"It's like hydrophobia, but worse."

"Oh."

"Get the Playtex Living Glove," I instructed Gracie, hoping it would be tooth-proof.

Sensing that something terrible was afoot, Carvel began to hobble slowly away. She rolled like a one-legged sailor in a storm, but when she was almost out of the fort I scooped her up with one hand.

"Not so fast, me hardy," I said in my best imitation sea captain's voice. "You'll take your medicine or you'll walk the plank."

"I'm sorry she hurt your finger, Jack," Gracie said returning with the yellow glove. "But don't be mad at her. She's didn't mean it."

"I don't know," I said. "Once they get the taste of human flesh...."

"Jack!"

"All right, let's try it again," I said. "Except this time, you do it. She's your cat, not mine."

I got Gracie to sit on the floor and placed the kitten in her arms.

"Pet her for a while to calm her down. And here, see if she'll eat something."

I ripped open a bag of dry cat food and took out a few pieces of reddish stuff. It had no smell, and probably no nutritional value, but it was vet approved. If I had been a cat, I would have preferred steak, tuna fish, or even mouse.

Gracie had no hesitation about sticking her fingers into Carvel's mouth and depositing a piece of food on the kitten's tongue. Carvel gagged, then chewed, just as Gracie retracted her fingers.

"She likes it," Gracie trilled.

"Give her a few more pieces," I said. "Then I'll hide the pill in the food."

With the skill of a surgeon, I inserted the white pill in the maroon food cube and squeezed the edges together.

"Here, give her this," I told Gracie, handing her the potent pellet. "She'll never know what hit her."

I was wrong, because when Gracie put the piece of food in Carvel's mouth, the kitten cocked her head, looked puzzled, and then spit it out with a distinct *ptoot*. She wasn't fooled a bit.

"Give her some more food," I said, "and see if she'll eat it."

Gracie complied and the kitten, with her anti-medicine radar, greedily gobbled it down. Satisfied she wouldn't reject being fed, I used a glass to crush the pill into powder and put half in a piece of cat food, thinking that the kitten wouldn't be able to detect a smaller amount of penicillin. Gracie tried again, but Carvel couldn't be tricked. She spat it out and looked up at me with contempt.

"Yew," she said, the cat equivalent to "yuck."

"This is ridiculous," I said, sitting on the cement floor. I outweighed the kitten by 170 pounds and was twice as smart—well, maybe one-and-a-half times as smart—but I could not get a tiny pill down her gullet. There was only one solution, I reasoned. Brute force would have to do.

"Wrap her in the blanket, Gracie," I said, with sudden resolve, "and hold on tight."

I got on my knees above the confined kitten and stared into her amber eyes, trying to hypnotize her into compliance. She looked at me with a combination of fear and anger, daring me to try something. I put on the yellow rubber glove and jacked open her jaws; then, with the thumb and forefinger of my other hand, I plinked the pill down her throat. Carvel let out a gacking sound, but the pill remained inside her.

"Take that," I said. "Might makes right."

Carvel looked at me reproachfully, knowing she had lost the battle, but there was still a war to be fought.

"You have to have water with a pill," Gracie said.

"Then let's see if she'll drink," I said.

I had swiped three pea-green bowls from the back of a kitchen cabinet. My father had received four of them as an inducement to fill up the Dodge at the opening of a new service station in town. Somehow, he had thought he would be getting fine china for his five bucks, because he was dashed when he opened the box to reveal cheapo plastic. For days, he had been remorseful that he had jilted his regular gas station attendant for a stranger offering tawdry gifts. However, bilious green or not, they were perfect for Carvel's food, water, and milk bowls. Nobody would ever miss them.

I filled a bowl with water from the laundry sink and placed it on the floor of the fort.

"Put her next to it," I said to Gracie.

The kitten looked at the water for a moment, but she didn't do anything.

"Go on, Carvel," Gracie said. "Drink it."

Carvel looked at her expectantly, but didn't make a move.

"Like this," Gracie said, crawling over to the bowl and lapping up some water.

Carvel watched this ludicrous scene and, although I know it is impossible, I swear she was laughing at Gracie. I certainly was.

"See?" Gracie said, her face dripping. "It's easy."

Carvel rolled her eyes and smirked; then she bent over and casually scooped up a few tonguefuls, implying that any idiot knew how to drink water.

"She's so smart, Jack," Gracie said.

"Yeah, but I don't think we are," I said. "So far, she's gotten us to save her life, lie to Mom and Dad, take her to the vet, hide her away down here, and feed and water her. In return, she has eaten two of my fingers, given me rabies, and made you get down on your hands and knees like a dummy and drink water from a bowl. Who's smarter?"

And Carvel had done all that while she was at death's door. What lay ahead of us when she felt better? I wondered.

"What?" Gracie asked, wiping her face with a grubby hand.

"She's tortured us enough for one morning," I said. "Let's leave her be."

❋ 🎄 ❋

After a few days of unprofessional care, Carvel was obviously feeling better. Her eyes were brighter, her wounds were healing, and she spent less time sleeping and more time exploring her new home. I had enough confidence in Gracie to let her ram a penicillin pill down the kitten twice a day, glad to be rid of that task. Carvel didn't seem to have the same craving for Gracie's flesh as she did for mine.

In my unprofessional opinion, the cat still didn't drink enough liquids, but she developed two odd habits that made me forget to monitor her intake. The first one gave us quite a scare.

I arrived home late one afternoon after playing four hours of half-court basketball. I was looking forward to a hot shower and a cool party that night. But before I could even take off my coat, Gracie streaked out of my room and grabbed me by the arm.

"Come quick," she whispered.

"What's the matter?" I asked.

"I thought you'd never get here," she said, dragging me to the door to the basement.

"Where are you going, Gracie?" my mother called from the kitchen.

"Just to the fort," she said. "I want Jack to help me with something."

"Don't stay all day down there. Dinner is in a half-hour."

At the bottom the stairs, Gracie burst into tears.

"She's gone, Jack. Carvel has run away," she sobbed.

"Have you looked for her?"

"Everywhere, but I can't find her. Where is she?"

The windows were small, high, and locked, and it seemed unlikely that a kitten with a gimpy leg could negotiate the rickety stairs and escape into the house.

"She's got to be here somewhere," I said. "Let's just sit down and think about this."

Gracie sat next to me and put her head on my shoulder while I looked around the bleak basement. The washer and dryer were both top loaders, too far off the ground for Carvel—unless she was some kind of Olympic high jumper. There was a pile of discarded furniture in one corner, but I could see that none of the chairs or tables were occupied by a marmalade cat. In the other corner were a bunch of cardboard boxes that housed the Christmas tree ornaments—a possible hiding place. But a thorough search revealed no sleeping kitten tangled in tinsel.

"Damn," I said.

"She hates me," Gracie said.

"Hey," I said, putting my arm around her. "She's just a kitten. I'm sure she loves you very much."

"Then why isn't she here?"

The basement lights suddenly flickered off and on—my mother's signal that dinner was ready—and out of the corner of my eye, I saw something glow in the darkness.

"Gracie, run up the stairs and turn out the lights," I said.

"Why?"

"Just do it."

She clumped up the wooden stairs and the basement was plunged into darkness. I saw what I thought I had seen.

"Turn 'em on and come down here," I said.

"And now, ladies and gentleman, for your edification and entertainment, I shall produce a pussycat out of the thin air," I said when Gracie returned.

"Don't tease me, Jack," Gracie said.

"Who's teasing? Watch this."

I pretended to roll up my sleeves, waved my arms around like the magicians on the *Ed Sullivan Show*, and said, "Abracadabra!"

"Where is she?" Gracie asked, looking around, apparently expecting a puff of smoke. "I don't see her."

"Go check the stove," I said.

"I already did," Gracie said.

"Try the bottom part."

Gracie reluctantly walked over to the abandoned stove and bent down.

"Mew," Carvel said.

Gracie pulled the kitten from the broiler and hugged her with almost enough force to crush the life out of the poor animal.

"Carvel, I love you," Gracie said, nuzzling the surprised kitten. "You're back, you're back!"

"Would you come on," my mother yelled down the stairs. "Dinner's on the table."

"Just a minute, Mom," I called back. "We'll be right there."

"Jack, how did you do that?" Gracie asked me, her eyes full of wonder.

"Magic," I said.

"Thank you," she said, wrapping her arms around me. "You're the bestest brother."

Also the bestest liar, I thought. There was no magic involved. I had seen the kitten's glowing eyes in the stove when the lights had gone out.

"Gracie! Get up here now!" Mother shouted down the stairs. "Jack!"

We had to bow to the inevitable.

That evening, after dinner, I moved the stove into Gracie's fort. Now both kitten and kid had forts of their own. The cat liked the security of curling up at the back of the broiler and watching her limited world with great intensity. Gracie put Carvel's blanket in with her and gave her the rubber mouse I had purchased at great cost. Carvel took one look at the toy and freaked out. She screeched and spit and finally batted it out of the stove like a hockey player. So much for Gracie's pronouncement that Carvel liked toys, I thought. But she did like Gracie. Extravagantly. The little kitten soon became a part of my sister—almost literally.

The next day I witnessed the first scaling of Mt. Gracie, which happened while I was applying salve to the kitten's burns. Carvel was lying complacently in my hand, allowing me to slather her with the foul-smelling ointment when I must have hit an especially sore spot. She screeched, wrenched herself from my grip, limped over to Gracie, and climbed her like a tree. After a few seconds of circling, Carvel settled on Gracie's shoulder, her face peeking out from behind my sister's hair. She was like a miniature lion peering through the tall grass looking for prey. Mt. Gracie, of course, erupted into uncontrollable giggles.

From that time on, if Gracie was in the basement, you could be sure that Carvel was on her shoulder. It was as if my sister had grown a second—feline—head. They hopped, skipped, danced, and jumped rope together, Carvel hanging on for dear life. They looked at pictures, entertained at tea parties, and sang songs together. They drew pictures, painted, and had long, intimate conversations. I don't know for sure that Carvel was having a good time, but I had never seen my sister happier. She positively radiated joy and contentment.

The change in my little sister didn't go unnoticed.

"I'm worried about Gracie," my mother said one morning. "She seems so happy."

"Call the police," I said in mock alarm. "We can't let this go on. What would the neighbors think?"

"Wise guy," my mother said. "She spends all her time in the fort and never bothers me or asks me to play with her anymore."

"Let me get this straight. You miss sitting around for hours talking to stuffed animals?" I said. "You're losing it, Mom."

"Something's not right," she said. "A mother knows."

Thank goodness you don't know, I thought.

"She also talks to herself," Mom continued. "Sometimes I swear there is someone in the basement with her."

"Probably an imaginary friend," I ventured.

"Imaginary friends are cute at three," she said. "Worrisome at six."

"Get her a shrink," I said.

My mother made a face indicating she didn't approve of Freudian analysis.

"Speaking of shrink, Gracie, well—how do I put this gently?—stinks. She smells like she's been playing at a garbage dump all day."

The awful-smelling salve, I thought, but before I could think up a rational excuse for Gracie's malodorous emanations, Gracie herself made an unscheduled appearance.

"Mommy, are you getting me any presents for

Christmas?" she asked.

"Of course, dear," my mother said.

"Well, you don't have to," Gracie said. "I have everything I want."

Then she skipped out of the kitchen singing tunelessly to herself.

"See?" my mother said. "That's not normal."

"Maybe she's inherited your, uh, Christmas spirit," I said lamely.

"If you look up the word *greed* in the dictionary, you'll find it illustrated with the picture of a six-year-old," Mom said. "When you and Evan were her age, you wanted every toy at F.A.O. Schwarz—and that was just for stocking stuffers. At six, after opening so many presents your arms hurt, you growled at me, 'That all?'"

Not knowing how to reply, I grunted and escaped. If Sherlock Moms was on the case, we were probably in big trouble.

Part II

December 18-23, 1962

CHAPTER 7

The kitten lay in the darkness of the old stove trying to understand where she was and what had happened to her. All she knew was that she was hurt, hurt bad, and there was a monstrous foreign object attached to her leg. When she tried to walk, it got in her way. But as hard as she tried to shake it off, it wouldn't budge. She didn't know that without the splint she wouldn't be able to walk at all.

She crawled deeper into the broiler and tried to make herself disappear from sight. Her instinct told her that this was a safe place because nothing could sneak up on her from behind and she had a good view out the front. So far, though, she had had only two visitors: the big one and the small one.

Although they both hurt her sometimes, there didn't seem to be any anger in their eyes. Far from it. They whispered soft words to her, even as they tried to get her to swallow awful-tasting things and covered her with foul-smelling grease that made her nose quiver in disgust. But they made up for those times by giving her something wonderful. It was soft and chewy and delicious. Every time the little one tore open a paper bag, out would come the food she had craved for so long. Fearing that the flow of this life-giving substance would suddenly be cut off, the kitten made sure she ate all she could, stuffing herself until she felt sick. Then she wanted more. She never knew when this banquet would end.

The big one and the small one liked to hold her, but that made her uncomfortable. She had never been stroked or petted before and it was strange for her. She kept waiting for them to hurt her, but most of the time they were content to rub their hands over her head and back and leave the sore spots alone. The kitten soon discovered that if she submitted to this odd behavior, they would feed her, and that was enough for her to remember not to bite them or claw them—most of the time.

Then one day, the big one had hurt her and she had shrieked with pain. Thinking only to get away from him, she had blundered into the small one and, using her claws, climbed up the fuzzy red sweater until she found herself entangled in the material. Pulling free, she hid behind the small one's hair, looking out for her attacker. The little one made a funny sound and rubbed her head against the kitten's body, not in a threatening way, but softly, gently. Still wary, the kitten cuddled up to the small one and mewed in her ear. That brought more funny sounds. Satisfied she was secure, the kitten settled down and observed what was going on from her perch high on the little one's shoulder. Now she had two safe places to hide.

The kitten enjoyed being carried around so high up in the air and, even when the little one made jerky movements that threatened to knock her off, the kitten simply dug in with her claws until the room stopped spinning. She much preferred for the little one to sit still and play quietly. It was those times when the kitten seemed to relax the most and was able to doze contentedly.

Every morning, just as the sun came up, she would find herself waiting impatiently for the little one to return. She knew she would get food, but she also missed the soft voice in her ear and the gentle touch on her head. The kitten didn't like the wet kisses on her mouth, but she abided them with aggravated resignation.

In her short life, the kitten had known terror, pain, hunger, and isolation. Now she was feeling something new, something she had never felt before. It was called love, but, of course, she had no way of knowing that.

CHAPTER 8

Christmas comes but once a year...and it's probably a good thing, too. At sixteen, I didn't know if I could take the pressure if that day arrived, say, every two months. It was not that I was curmudgeonly before my time. It was that I found my family's holiday rituals to be peculiar, wearisome, and, increasingly, a drain on my valuable teenage time.

For example, there was tree buying. Normal people found a fir at a local dealer and brought it home. Not my father. He had a secret supplier of pines located miles and miles away in another state. That meant just getting there and back was an all-day affair. So every year, with monotonous regularity, he would take the day off from work just to make the trek. Why a tree from that particular location was superior to any other, I never knew. But my father swore by Lenny's Evergreen Emporium, which was hidden somewhere in the wilds of New Jersey.

Evan and Gracie were enthusiastic tree buyers and even my mother didn't mind the ride, but the thought of spending an entire day cooped up with my family made me wince. I felt I was too mature to be seen in public with my parents. But if I tried to back out of the journey, my father would sigh meaningfully, my mother would shake her head sadly and say that she didn't know how many more Christmases we would all spend together, and Gracie would burst into tears. Faced with that combined emotional assault, I would always cave in like the spineless creature I was.

The only saving grace that year was that my father let me drive the Chrysler 300 with its 800 horsepower engine or whatever it was. That was quite a treat after all the hours I spent coaxing the Dodge along at a pace that would have made a snail laugh.

"Slow down," my father commanded when we hit the highway. "We're not going to a fire."

"Too bad," I said. "We'd get there first."

But I slowed to seventy-five for safety's sake.

Once we finally made it to the Evergreen Emporium, my father began his annual inspection tour of the grounds, presumably looking for the perfect tree. There were hundreds of fir trees lined up by size and type and it should have been easy to choose one. But my father insisted on personally looking over the entire inventory. On the way, he would make inane comments like, "Too small." "Too big." "Not full enough." Why he wasted so much time belaboring the obvious baffled me until I noticed that Gracie and Evan were following him around like puppies, hanging on his every boring word. He was doing it for them, I thought, not because he's dumb. That was a revelation to me.

My brother and sister were running all over the lot and calling his attention to various trees. Dad would stop his leisurely pace and make a show of examining their favorites, discuss the pros and cons with them, and then move on. He was dragging out the process to amuse and entertain them, I thought. Of course, he had done the same thing with me for years and I remembered I had loved every minute of it. But at that moment, all I wanted to do was get on with the purchase and get home.

I set a new record that day, cutting almost two hours off the usual round trip, causing my father's knuckles to go white. Then I tried to make myself invisible while the usual argument over Christmas tree decorating erupted. From the fuss they made, you would have thought that Evan, Gracie, and my father were top designers in a national competition. The three of them had definite ideas about what a perfectly decked out tree should look like and each of them thought the others were untalented rubes and boobs.

"No, Daddy. Not there. Down lower where you can see it," Gracie wailed.

"You have to put the lighter decorations on top and the heavier ones on the branches that can support them," my father countered reasonably.

"That looks like dog vomit," Evan said sourly.

"Ewww," Gracie cried.

"Evan!" my mother called from the kitchen, where she was wisely monitoring the feud, not participating in it.

They went through this routine with each of the hundreds of ornaments and decorations we stored in the basement most of the year. The sniping, quibbling, and squabbling went on for hours and made me wish I was adopted and that my real family was coming to get me soon.

When the tiresome trio had finally finished decorating the tree—to their mutual dissatisfaction—it was tinsel time.

"Can I help this year?" Gracie asked.

"Only if you do it my way," my father said.

"But it takes *sooo* long," Gracie whined.

"A job worth doing is worth doing well," my father intoned portentously.

"I'm going to watch TV," Evan said, showing more sense than I would have imagined, for Dad was the Tchaikovsky of tinsel—a maestro who organized random strips of aluminum into a shimmering symphony. He put the foil on one piece at a time, adjusting his work as he went along, and his technique produced absolutely magnificent results. Dad could make any ratty tree shine like the one in Rockefeller Center. I always admired the final outcome, but I couldn't be bothered wasting four hours of my limited time to go a-tinseling. Besides, although he complained loudly and often, I think my father secretly enjoyed doing the job unencumbered by noisy, sloppy kids.

"I'm going to play with my—in my fort," Gracie said.

"Why don't you come and help me make Christmas cookies instead?" my mother called from the kitchen.

"Oh, no," I said. "The Curse of the Whitleys."

Whitley was my mother's maiden name and she had inherited a recipe for sugar cookies from her great-grandmother. I gathered it was a secret recipe because Mom kept it hidden away between the pages of a book of poetry until she needed it to make everyone's life poetically miserable.

That's not quite accurate. The cookies only ruined the lives of my mother and the kid she chose to help her. As the oldest, I had been drafted at the age of four to mix, stir, and bake. It was a chore I dreaded each year—like cleaning out the gutters and putting up the storm windows. Finally, I rebelled and Evan was conscripted to do the dirty work. Now, apparently, he was off the hook and it was Gracie's turn to suffer.

How could a bunch of cookies cause so much trouble? Because my mother took the obligation of making them with a religious seriousness. She derived no pleasure from baking—she didn't even eat cookies—but she felt a tremendous pressure to fulfill a family tradition. Mom had never missed a year and she wasn't about to, regardless of wars, natural disasters, or acts of God. Only death could stop her. Even then, she expected someone to carry on in her absence.

With grim determination, my mother lined up the ingredients, swept back her hair, and plunged into the mysteries of the cursed cookies. The dough came first. It contained more butter than a herd of cows and it had to be kept cold at all times. If the dough grew warm, it would melt into a sticky mess and became unusable. Many a time I had watched my mother's face turn red as the pale dough dissolved into a gelatinous mass. To avoid this tragedy, she put the dough on the windowsill to keep it cold.

Once at the proper temperature, the dough had to be rolled and rolled and then rolled some more. Then there was time to cut out only four or five cookies—a tree, an angel, a snowman, a wreath, and a bell—before the dough went into its melting routine again. Back it went to the windowsill. This laborious toil went on for hours, but yielded only a meager crop of thin cookies because during baking about half of them would burn. Row after row of charred and inedible Father Christmases had to be laid to rest unceremoniously in the garbage.

Gracie dutifully joined my mother in the kitchen and they started the familiar ritual of incorporating the sticks of butter with the pounds of flour. I watched idly as Mom put the dough in a bowl and placed it on the sill. That's when it struck me.

"Why don't you put the dough in the refrigerator?" I asked.

"I don't know," my mother said. "I'm just following the recipe. That's why it says you can only make these cookies when it's cold outside."

"If the recipe said for you to jump off a bridge, would you do it?" I asked, paraphrasing one of Mom's favorite phrases.

"Wise guy," she said, wiping the flour from her brow.

"Seriously, Mom," I said. "Just how old is this recipe, anyway?"

"Well, let's see," she said. "Sometime around the Civil War, I think."

"Stop me if I'm wrong," I said. "General Grant didn't have a refrigerator, did he?"

"No."

"So, you could make these cookies on the Fourth of July—using the refrigerator to cool the dough," I said.

"Twice a year? What a horrible thought," my mother said.

"Mom, come quick!" Gracie yelled.

We went over to the window in time to see a squirrel doing a tap dance in the bowl of dough. He would lift one foot and then another, trying to escape a gluey death.

"Shoo," my mother said.

"Go away!" Gracie shouted.

The squirrel looked at them sadly and continued his sticky dance, no doubt thinking he was trapped and would soon sink to his death. I opened the window and pried the beast out of the bowl with a wooden spoon and sent him on his way.

"I rest my case," I said smugly.

"For me, these cookies are Christmas," my mother said wistfully. "If I don't follow the recipe precisely, I'm afraid the cookies would lose their...panache."

"They'd also lose their squirrel sh—"

"Jack!" my mother and Gracie said simultaneously.

I left the kitchen shaking my head. As a modern, up-to-date teenager, I held all forms of tradition in contempt, feeling that, like the cookies, they came from a dumber, out-of-it era, and the sooner these customs were abandoned, the better off the world would be. Horses, for example, were fine animals, but if I wanted to go to California, I would have preferred to ride a Boeing 707, then the newest jet airliner around. People like my parents were hopelessly locked into the past and insisted on dragging me with them—on spruce buying sprees, tree decorating skirmishes, and infernal cookie-making schemes.

But of all the Christmas traditions, the one that gave me fits was buying presents. I was hopelessly inept.

"What are you going to get Gracie for Christmas?" my mother asked me the next morning.

"Uh," I said expansively.

As an expert translator of teenage lingo, Mom took that to mean, "I don't know. What would you suggest?" So she made a few recommendations, none of which appealed to me. Dolls, I knew, were out of the question. Except for a favored few, Gracie just stripped them down to the bare plastic and stacked their naked bodies like cordwood in the corner of her room. Stuffed animals appealed to her more, but while she wore the fabric off her two favorites—a cat and a tiger—the other four thousand gathered dust in the closet. Games were not her forte either because she refused to play by the rules and insisted on making up her own as the game progressed. That led to a family boycott of Candy Land and Sorry! What to get her? As usual, I was at a loss.

Buying presents had always been a chore for me, mostly because I hadn't wanted anything for myself since I had begged for a Hopalong Cassidy cap pistol when I was six.

That's not to say I was some kind of St. Francis, casting aside all worldly goods. Far from it. I lusted after a British racing green Triumph TR-4, two weeks on the beach in Hawaii, and a modest-size airplane. But I couldn't think of anything I wanted that cost less than three thousand dollars or would fit inside a hanging stocking. Worse, I didn't have the imagination to come up with ten-dollar treasures that would make other people happy or at least satisfied.

Sometimes, however, I got lucky. Evan had suddenly blossomed into a star soccer player. As an ardent football fan and player, I took a dim view of that turn of events, but a Rawlings soccer ball was an easy choice. Dad was impossible to buy for. In my younger and stupider days, I had gotten him a deluxe Simonize kit. He loved it—so much so that he made me polish about forty of his cars. After that, he got ties, socks, and handkerchiefs.

Mom was even more annoying in the present purchasing department. Every year she insisted that she didn't want anything—except some homemade trinket we were to make for her. That resulted in a procession of Styrofoam tree ornaments with glitter inscriptions, ragged clay animals, badly nailed trinket boxes, and the occasional hand-loomed pot holder.

That year, I decided to test Mom's homespun preferences by hiring the little brother of a friend of mine to make an ashtray for me in art class. The boy had done a stellar job producing a pumpkin-sized, pumpkin-colored creation. Oddly, although he had used fifty pounds of clay, the tray for the ashes was only the size and depth of his nine-year-old finger. The result was useless and hideous— the perfect gift only a mother could profess to love. I doubled the kid's commission to a buck.

"Why don't I get Gracie a cat?" I said.

After all, I knew where I could get one cheap.

My mother threw back her head and laughed and laughed.

"That's a good one," she said, wiping a tear from her eye.

I took that to mean "no" and I went back being perplexed.

"I've got it," I said, finally. "A book about cats."

"Great," my mother said. "Your father's not allergic to books and Gracie could use the practice."

In a house of compulsive readers, little Gracie was an oddity. Despite the best efforts of teachers, parents, and me, she didn't seem to get it. Her skills were poor and she professed to hate reading. Perhaps a book about her favorite subject would get her into the groove, I reasoned, or at least wipe out the last blank on my Christmas list.

I walked down to the local book shop that morning and rummaged around in the children's section looking for something I thought Gracie might like. I found it almost immediately—*The Compleat Book of Cats for Children* by Ruby L. Johnson. Although I was leery about any book that had a misspelling in the title, I thumbed through it, glad to see that the print was large and simple to read and there seemed to be an illustration on almost every page. So I plunked down my money, took one look at the huge line for wrapping, and left the shop. The less time I spent in any store, the better I liked it.

"What's in the bag?" Gracie asked when I found her in the basement.

Carvel gave me a perfunctory *mew* from her perch on Gracie's shoulder.

"An early Christmas present for you," I said.

"For me? For me?" she squealed, clapping her hands and executing a little dance, almost dislodging Carvel from her precarious roost.

Mom had been right about six-year-olds, I thought. Gracie almost attacked me to get at the shopping bag.

"Slow down," I said, fending her off. "And sit over there by your baby carriage."

When she and Carvel had taken their seat, I produced the large royal purple volume.

"Oh, it's just a book," Gracie said, disappointed.

"Yeah," I said. "But it's a book about kitties."

"Really?"

"Have a look."

I opened the book and spread it in her lap.

"Oh, there's a pretty one," she said admiring a picture of an Abyssinian. "And there's a beautiful white one."

"What kind of cat is the white one?" I asked.

"Sia, sia, mean," Gracie said trying to sound out the word in the caption.

"Sia is right," I said. "Use the *mmm* sound."

"Sia-mmm-mean."

"Close," I said. "What's that one?"

"Mainey coon cat," she said.

"Very good, except you don't pronounce the *e* in Maine. It's the state," I said.

"Like Vermount?"

"Kinda. Here, we'll read it together," I said.

We started from the very beginning, which was a mistake. The book was dedicated to Mr. Snuffles, the author's cat, and that set Gracie off. She immediately wanted to know what Mr. S. looked like, where he slept, what he ate, and his exact relationship with his mistress, Ruby L. Johnson. Faced with the unknowable, I had two options: lie or profess ignorance. So I lied. "Mr. Snuffles is eight years old, lives in a special white wicker basket in Ruby L. Johnson's kitchen, is black with white feet, and was found as a kitten in the city of Burlington, Vermount," I said, trying to cover all bases.

"What does he eat?" Gracie asked.

"Table scraps," I said.

"Jack! Cats don't eat tables. That's silly."

"I guess. But he's a pretty silly cat."

Not up to a grilling about copyright law, I skipped that page and got right to the origins of cats.

"Read this," I said, pointing to the opening paragraph.

"Cats were dom-i-cated more than five hundred? thousand? years ago. The E- E- E- E- Egg—"

"Egyptians," I said. "You know, the pyramid guys."

"Egyptians kep-ted them as house-held pets and left paintings of them on the walls," Gracie read, slowly moving her finger along the page.

"See, there's a painting of an Egyptian cat," I said.

"It's not very good, is it? I like this other one better," Gracie said flipping through the book and finding a photograph of a fat tomcat.

Although I despaired of her ever becoming an art critic or an archeologist, Gracie did a credible job of reading the first paragraph in less than fifteen minutes—the exact time it took my patience to evaporate. As she launched into paragraph two, I suddenly notice a peculiar and unpleasant odor.

"What's that smell?" I asked Gracie, who was sounding out the word "history."

Gracie shrugged.

"Where's it coming from?"

"Over there behind the furnace," she said. "Carvel goes poopy there."

"But I set up a litter box," I said.

"I told her to use it, but she didn't listen," Gracie said.

I spent the next half-hour cleaning and scrubbing Carvel's little presents. I used Dutch Cleanser, Clorox, and Tide to kill the smell, but in the process I made the stink stink worse. Even Carvel must have been nauseated by the odor, because she deserted Gracie's shoulder and scurried across the basement to hide amidst the discarded furniture.

"Pee-yew," Gracie said, holding her nose.

"I wonder how we get her to use the litter box?" I said, waving the foul air around with my hand. "Let's see. You showed her how to drink water from a bowl."

Gracie looked at me, her face suddenly registering the impact of my words.

"Jack!" she said. "I'm not going to poop in that box!"

"Then we'll have to find another way."

I opened two of the windows and turned on a small fan to blow the noxious fumes away. Soon I had a shivering child and a shivering kitten huddled together for warmth. But the winter winds did a good job returning the basement to its usual damp laundry smell.

"Put Carvel back in her fort and let's go upstairs," I said to Gracie. "I've got an idea."

When we had settled into the living room, I prepped Gracie on my plan.

"Don't blow it," I warned her. Then I nudged her when Mom came into the room.

"Mommy, how do cats go to the bathroom?" Gracie asked, her face shining with innocence.

"Why do you want to know?" my mother asked.

"Jack was reading to me about kitties, but it doesn't say how they go poopy."

"Outdoor cats go outside and indoor cats use a litter box," my mother said. "Jack knows that."

I shrugged and tried to look as innocent as Gracie.

"Do they know how to flush?" Gracie asked.

"You don't have to flush a litter box. The cat just scratches everything under the sand," she said.

"Scratches?" Gracie asked.

"Yes, like this," my mother said, curling her fingers and scratching like a cat.

I couldn't help it. I laughed out loud.

My mother gave me a withering look.

"But how do they know how?" Gracie insisted. "Do 'Gyptian cats know how?"

"Why all the sudden interest in cat elimination techniques?" my mother asked suspiciously.

"The book," I said, holding it up.

"Well, all you have to do is take their front paws in your hands and scratch for them," she said. "After a time or two, they'll get the idea. Then they won't go anywhere else."

"Oh," Gracie said. "Thanks, Mommy."

"Yeah, thanks," I said. "But I want to see you do your scratching impression again, Mom. Really."

She didn't dignify that remark with an answer and stalked out of the room.

"I think she's mad," Gracie said in a worried voice.

"Probably," I said. "But at least we got the answer. Go downstairs and scratch Carvel's paws in the litter and see if she's as smart as we think she is."

After Gracie had rushed off on her training mission, I turned on the tree lights and watched as the precisely placed tinsel seemed to ripple, flow, and change color—from silver to blue to green to violet—in the weak winter sunshine. Dad had transformed the tree into a first-class work of art, I thought, wondering why he had even bothered. Then I remembered him taking the day off from work to follow Gracie and Evan around Lenny's, patiently explaining the finer points of pine purchasing to them, and I suddenly realized that my father was a whole lot nicer of a person than I was or ever would be. He had gone to great trouble to give them a Christmas memory they would keep for the rest of their lives.

Despite myself, I had to admit that some traditions were better than others. I just hoped no one saw me admiring the tree or heard me say something nice about my father. That would have ruined the worldly image I was working on so diligently. Then I chomped into a Curse of the Whitleys, determined to ignore such old-fashioned thoughts.

CHAPTER 9

I could almost see the wind as it tormented the bare trees, making them creak and crack and bend and wave. The temperature was hovering around twenty-five degrees and there was the smell of snow in the air. In all, it was a perfect gray day to waste a few hours doing absolutely nothing, except being glad I had nowhere in particular to go. The house was quiet—everybody was out on various errands— and I reveled in the solitude. If only they would all go out more often, I thought, how much better life would be.

Having enjoyed *A Farewell to Arms*, I was deep into reading Hemingway's *The Sun Also Rises* when the phone rang. Expecting one of my friends to be on the line, I answered, "Jake's Pool Hall."

Silence.

"Hello?" I said.

A high-pitched, oddly familiar voice asked for my mother.

"She's not here," I said. "Can I take a message?"

"I want Jack to fix my television antenna. It blew down last night," Miss Langley said. "I'll miss my stories."

Well, too damn bad, I thought.

"I'll tell her," I said, having no intention of doing so.

What a lot of nerve, I thought, hanging up on one of the many banes of my existence. Why couldn't she leave me alone? Was I some sort of slave to be summoned at will and worked to death? I spent the next half-hour hatching hare-brained schemes of revenge, but my bloody reveries were interrupted by Mom and Gracie bursting into the house, their arms laden with packages and boxes.

"I ran into Miss Langley," my mother said, depositing her load on the chair next to me.

"Did you crush her?" I asked hopefully.

"She wants to see you, Jack," Gracie said, confirming the bad news.

"She said she left a message with someone," my mother continued.

"Probably Evan," I said, blaming the brother who hadn't been home all morning.

Mom then told me what I already knew and, seeing my sour expression, she launched into a lecture about the meaning of Christmas, the duty of the strong to help the weak, the concept of neighborliness, and a bunch of other things I had heard every December since I was two. Talk about words falling on barren ground. I became more and more furious at the injustice of it all.

"Why doesn't she just call a TV repairman like a normal person?" I asked heatedly.

"She probably can't afford to," my mother said.

"You're the one who always says that if you can't afford something, do without," I said, slinging Mom's words back in her face. "Let her listen to the radio."

Or eat cake, I thought, recalling my scant knowledge of the French Revolution. Suddenly, I realized I was having a revolution of my own.

"Jack, what's wrong with you?" my mother asked, genuinely puzzled. "It's Christmas."

For Mom, with her extravagant sense of holiday spirit, Christmas was enough to make the lion lie down with the lamb and Miss Langley turn into a kindly old lady.

"I don't care if it's Election Day," I said. "I'm not going to do it."

"Please," Gracie said, grabbing my arm and looking up at me. "Miss Langley gives me cookies."

"She gives me a pain in the—"

"Jack!" Mom and Gracie said in one voice, knowing I wasn't thinking "neck."

"I'll go with you," Gracie said, as if that might make a difference. "She's such a nice lady. Please, please, pretty please?"

That word again, I thought, looking at Gracie's expectant face, her round cheeks still red from the cold. She looked so trusting that I grudgingly gave in—like the craven coward I was. But I was not going to go gently into that unsweet afternoon.

"This is the last damn time!" I roared.

Then I made a show of storming around the house looking for my jacket. I ripped through the closet, flinging coats and sweaters out of the way and cursing the weakness of my spine. By now, I was madder at myself than the irritating Miss Langley and that made everything worse. I had the presence of mind to grab a screwdriver, but my revolution had fizzled and I was on the run. I managed, however, to slam the front door with enough force to unseat the wreath and rattle the windows, so at least my parting shot was a good one.

I didn't even feel the winter wind as I stalked murderously toward the source of my discontent—the woman who had wrecked my morning and probably my entire day with her unreasonable demands. My size eleven boots ruthlessly trampled the crunchy snow, grinding it into powder. If I had lived in Tokyo, I would have made a stellar stand-in for Godzilla.

As I approached her house, I saw Miss Langley's white hair bobbing up and down in the window of her kitchen. She was probably doing a jig, I thought, and laughing at me. When I rang the bell, she jerked open the door and said, "It's up there."

"What?" I asked softly, knowing full well she was talking about the antenna on the roof.

"What?" Miss Langley said, cupping her ear.

"What?" I said, even more softly.

"On the roof, on the roof," she yelled, slamming the door in my face.

"You're welcome," I said.

I retrieved the aluminum ladder I had used to put up the tree lights and braced it against the side of the house. As I was pulling away, I caught the palm of my left hand on a jagged piece of metal and cursed loudly enough for even deaf Miss Langley to hear. I blotted the blood on my coat and started up the ladder, using my uninjured hand to grip the rungs. Twenty-five feet off the ground, I stepped gingerly onto the roof.

I could see two things immediately. First, Miss Langley needed new shingles. And second, the roof was covered with so much ice, it looked like a high, dangerous skating rink.

The antenna in question was made of steel, was about four feet long, and was shaped like a capital *H*. It was hanging toward me, but it was still a long way from my grasp. Figuring it was too dangerous to walk on the icy roof, I decided to crawl on my belly up the forty-five degree pitch. I took a breath, knowing it might be my last, and slowly inched my way toward the target, using my arms and legs to drag myself upward. I felt as if I were in a dream attempting to escape some unknown monster. But like dream running, I was not making much progress. The wind howled around me, threatening to pluck me off the roof and hurl me to the ground. All I could see were the frigid black shingles in front of my nose as I lunged forward, then slipped back, time after time. Just when I was about to give up, my hand touched freezing metal. It felt like fire.

I looked up to see that the antenna was bent and had shed one of its leads. The other one was lying nearby, occasionally flapping in the breeze like a half-dead snake. The guy wires were twisted, but intact. Using every bit of my strength, I hauled myself to the apex of the roof and straddled it, feeling sharp needles of ice, pushed by the vicious wind, rip at my face.

After I was secure, I grabbed the antenna and pulled it up to the top of the roof. From there, it was only a matter of slamming it back into its bracket and reattaching the loose lead. I also tightened the guy wires and tried to get the kink out of the base, without much success.

As I was admiring my work, I heard a muffled sound from below and saw Miss Langley waving at me furiously. Then she ran back inside the house. Figuring that the antenna was not properly adjusted, I turned it a few inches and waited. Miss Langley shot out of the house again, this time waving like an Olympic semaphore champion. I turned the antenna a few more inches and waited. And waited. No Miss Langley.

Finally, it dawned on me that she was sitting comfortably by her fireplace watching television while I was quickly solidifying into a large, ungainly weathervane on her roof. Disgusted, I unlocked my legs from the roof peak and I swear I could hear my bones creak and crack like the tree branches waving around me.

Now all I had to do was get down. That was the tricky part. I had to slide down the slippery roof backward and hit the gutter with my feet or I would plunge out into space and slam into the ground, breaking legs, arms, and head. They probably wouldn't find me until spring, I thought.

Taking a breath that burned like sandpaper in my throat, I began the descent as slowly as I could. My fingernails and elbows dug into the ice and I snowplowed my legs to slow me down. But I began to pick up speed. Too much speed. I grabbed the screwdriver, plunged it into the shingles, and held on for all I was worth.

I had always heard that your life flashes before your eyes when you are about to die and it's true. Visions of Diane wearing her bikini on the beach ran through my head as I hung there like an impaled insect. The rest of my life apparently didn't make the cut because the next thing I knew, my flailing boots hit the wooden gutter with a clunk. I lay there for a minute before inching my way over to the ladder and gratefully climbing back to earth.

"Nice try, Langley," I shouted, shaking my fist in the air. "But you can't kill me."

Then I walked slowly home, more scared than mad, and was greeted by Gracie who took one look at me and screamed for Mom.

"Oh, my God," my mother gasped.

I didn't think I looked *that* bad.

"Gracie, get the first aid kit. Jack, go wash," my mother said, taking command. Like most women, my mother was at her best when it came to injuries involving leaking bodily fluids. Frankly, the sight of someone else's blood makes me queasy and I would be useless trying to staunch a decent flow. But for some reason, my own blood gushing like Old Faithful never bothered me much. I washed my ruined hands with hot water, surprised that it felt tepid on my frozen skin. A few splashes of iodine and a couple of Band-Aids from the first-aid kit completed the course of treatment.

"What happened, Jack?" my mother asked with concern. "Were you in a fight?"

"With a roof and an antenna," I said.

"A roof?"

"Yeah, Mom. That's where they put antennas nowadays. It's the latest thing," I said.

"You mean you were crawling around Miss Langley's roof? In this weather? Without your gloves?"

I showed her my busted-up hands.

"I had no idea," she said, looking a bit pale. "I thought it was one of those things that sits on a television set."

"Rabbit ears," I said.

"Miss Langley has a rabbit?" Gracie asked, suddenly interested.

"Mom, I was fifty feet in the air and I almost fell about ten times," I said, exaggerating for effect. "There was ice all over the place, the wind was blowing a hundred miles an hour, and I could have broken my neck."

"That's why you didn't want to help her. It was too dangerous," my mother said, having a sudden reason that excused her hard-hearted son. "Really, Jack, I didn't know."

Of course I would have balked at fixing rabbit ears for Old Lady Langley, but I decided to play the put-upon martyr. It made me look like less of a jerk.

"A lot you care, sending me to an early grave," I said, prolonging the agony and throwing my favorite book title into the fray.

That did it. My mother spent fifteen minutes apologizing to me while I sat there enjoying every minute of it with a smug, self-righteous smile on my face. If being insufferable is a part of growing up, I was very good at that part. But I didn't have much chance to indulge that side of me because I was adept at staying out of my mother's way fifty weeks a year. It was only when she was suffused with the Christmas spirit that I ran afoul of her—witness my outburst that afternoon. The problem was that no matter how hard I tried, I couldn't match her faith in the goodness of mankind, especially if Miss Langley was included in that group.

"Can I go see the rabbit, please?" Gracie asked. "They're so cute."

Mom tried to explain the difference between rabbit ears and rabbits, but I don't think Gracie believed her. She kept asking questions until Mom suggested she go play somewhere.

"Come with me, Jack," Gracie said. "We can have a tea party."

"Not now," I said. "I'm too tired."

"Then I'll have to wait for Daddy to get home," Gracie said. "He *likes* to have tea parties."

Well, maybe, but Gracie was partially right. Dad was putty in her hands, always willing to play with her and indulge her in any way. They had a special relationship that excluded the rest of the family. Not that we minded. Dad took the pressure off the rest of us when it came to mind-numbing hours of tea party chatter and other silly games Gracie liked to play.

With Evan and me, Dad was much less demonstrative because he realized that ideal relations between teenage sons and their father were reflected in England's attitude toward her American colonies from the founding until the mid-eighteenth century—mainly, benign neglect. It was only when the colonial power became intrusive and demanding that the colonists rebelled. My father, who was a student of history, understood these dynamics. Certainly, he maintained an aloof foreign policy when it came to dealing with his sons. Oh, he groused from time to time just to let us know he was there, but generally he left us alone. At that stage in our lives, neglect was indeed benign, and we appreciated it.

With Gracie, however, Dad discarded all pretense of neutrality. She was his little girl and he doted on her. In turn, Gracie loved him beyond all calculation. My mother was there all the time for her, but Daddy was her birthday, Christmas, and the Fourth of July all rolled into one. In contrast, Mom was August 26—a Tuesday.

From the time she was a tiny baby, Dad had sung to her, read to her, and told her the most outrageous bedtime stories imaginable. He could make her giggle with a look and one word was enough to get her to go to bed, brush her teeth, or eat her vegetables—tasks she usually balked at with mule-like obstinacy. When he came home from work, Gracie invariably leapt to her feet with a shriek and ran into his arms, smothering him with kisses. Evan and I, if we even noticed his return, would wave languorously or grunt a greeting. But mostly, our eyes were glued to the television set.

That's why Gracie was so upset when my father dragged himself home from work that evening and announced that he was sick as a dog.

"I've felt lousy for a week and I don't know what's wrong with me," he said. "It must be the flu. I just can't stop sneezing and coughing."

"Poor Daddy," Gracie said and flung herself into his arms.

"Achoo," my father said.

I could see his nose was as red as his eyes, and I knew instantly what was wrong with him. He wasn't sick as a dog. He was sick as a cat. His allergy to cat dander, which had been slowly dragging him down, was kicking in with a vengeance.

"I'll take care of you, Daddy," Gracie said, putting her head on his shoulder.

"Thanks, sweetie, but I think I'll just take a nap before dinner," he said. "It seems to be getting worse now that I'm home."

Coughing, gagging, and sneezing, he retreated to his bedroom. Gracie looked worried and wrung her small hands together.

"I'm going to take care of Daddy," she said with determination.

"Leave him alone until he feels better," I said, knowing she would kill him with kisses.

I debated telling her that she was the cause of his illness, but decided that Gracie would be crushed. How could she choose between the two loves of her life? But I had a back-up plan, which I put into action immediately.

"Gracie, you've got to wash more," I said.

"I take a bath every night," she said.

"I know, but you've got to wash real good after every time you play with Carvel," I said.

"She's not dirty anymore," Gracie said, somewhat offended.

"No, but her salve smells terrible and Mom has noticed," I said.

"Oh no," Gracie said. "Do you think she knows?"

"She's getting suspicious," I said. "We've got to tell her soon."

"No, Jack, please," Gracie said, her lower lip beginning to tremble. "Not until after Christmas. Please?"

"Just wash then," I said sternly, hoping that she would get rid of cat dander as well as the smell of the salve. That ought to cure my father's allergy, I thought, wondering why I only got a *B* in biology when it was obvious that I was as brilliant as Louis Pasteur or Jonas Salk.

CHAPTER 10

Go tell Gracie it's dinnertime," my mother said as I drifted into the kitchen to see what was on the menu. The afternoon's exertions had made me so hungry I needed a couple of Whitley's Curses to tide me over.

"Gracie, dinner!" I shouted down the basement stairs.

"I could have done that," my mother said, giving me a pained look.

Then why didn't you? I wondered. Parents were so strange.

"Jack, go down there and see what she's doing," my mother said. "I heard her talking to herself again. Something about Carvel. That's ice cream, isn't it?"

"Soft ice cream. Maybe that's what she's serving at her tea party," I said, thinking fast.

"What an odd child," my mother said absently, but there was a look of concern on her face.

I found the odd child and her boon companion crawling around the floor of the fort. Gracie was giving Carvel pony rides and they both seemed to be enjoying themselves enormously.

"*Neeeeeeee,*" Gracie squealed, emitting a horse-like sound.

"You got to keep the noise down, Gracie," I said. "Mom can hear you."

The gallant steed froze in place.

"Is she coming down here?" Gracie asked, a look of alarm on her face.

"She will if you keep it up," I said. "Put the kitten back in the stove and let's go upstairs."

"You go ahead. I'll be right up. I don't want Mommy to find us."

As I was on my way, I noticed that the plant my mother kept in the basement looked distinctly bedraggled, even in the dim light. I inspected it and found that many of the lower leaves were ragged and torn. Chewed. There could be only one explanation: Carvel was eating the plant from the bottom up.

I had heard that cats and dogs will occasionally eat grass and plants when they were sick, but my mother would have a fit if this plant died. It was more than her favorite, it was the only one in the house she hadn't managed to kill. If it could live without light in the basement, apparently even Mom's black thumb couldn't destroy it. I couldn't let Carvel devour such a hearty survivor. My duty, as I saw it, was to use my gigantic scientific brain to find a solution to that vexing problem. But first, there was the matter of dinner.

We had fried chicken, mashed potatoes, and peas that evening and I inhaled everything on my plate and asked for more. Barely escaping death does that to me. I recounted my wild adventures on Miss Langley's roof, but my audience was unresponsive. Mom and Gracie had heard enough, Evan was unimpressed as only a younger brother can be, and my father could barely keep his swollen red eyes open. I shut up and concentrated on stuffing my face.

"Do you like ice cream?" my mother asked Gracie, filling the silence.

"Sure. Do we got some for dessert?"

"Not tonight, but maybe tomorrow," my mother said. "What kind do you like?"

"Vanilla."

"Yuck. That tastes like dog doo," Evan said.

"Ewww," Gracie said.

"Children!" my father warned, sneezing into his napkin.

"No, I mean what *type* of ice cream do you like?" my mother said, ignoring everything but her own ulterior motives. "Hard ice cream or soft ice cream?"

I knew where this was going and jumped in to save the day.

"You like Carvel, don't you?" I said pointedly.

"I love Carvel," Gracie said enthusiastically.

"You do?" Mom asked.

Realizing a bit late that Mom was talking about ice cream again, Gracie mumbled something unintelligible and focused her eyes on her lap. She was a great liar when she had the time to prepare her story, but as an impromptu fibber, she was as unconvincing as Mae West playing the Virgin Mary.

My mother made a *mmmm* sound, but I knew she was far from satisfied. I wouldn't have bought it either. I gazed around the room, trying not to make eye contact with anyone.

My father sat at the head of the table, his back to the living room. My mother was next to Gracie on the left, a position she had taken when Gracie was little and needed help feeding herself. Evan was on the right and I was opposite my father, having inherited Mom's original chair. The seating arrangements are important because I was the only one with an unobstructed view of the living room.

As I was glancing idly about, I saw, to my horror, Carvel, with her rolling three-legged gait, come strolling across the living room. She didn't seem to be in a hurry and stopped to glance at me with her usual curiosity. Then she continued on her journey, disappearing from sight and leaving me gagging on a chicken leg. Suddenly, she reversed her course, came back into view, and decided to pay me a visit. The closer she got, the more I seemed unable to move. But when she opened her mouth to meow and I finally sprang into action. I let out a loud cough to cover her noise, leaped to my feet, and hightailed it out of the dining room.

"Jack, where are you going?" my mother called after me.

I wasn't stopping for anything. Like a trick rider picking up a handkerchief from the ground at a full gallop, I scooped up Carvel in one smooth motion and got her out of sight of the others.

"I'll be right back," I yelled out from the basement steps, hoping no one had seen what I was really doing.

I hustled the kitten downstairs and shoved her in the broiler. This conspiracy stuff was getting more and more difficult by the minute. How had Carvel gotten up the stairs? I was sure that was impossible, but something was wrong, very wrong.

Returning to the table, I sat down and tried to look as if nothing had happened. That, of course, was impossible.

"Where did you disappear to?" my mother asked.

"Chicken bone," I lied, pointing to my throat. "I had to get it out."

My mother gave another of her patented "mmmm" sounds, indicating that she didn't believe me any more than she had believed Gracie's sudden interest in Carvel vanilla ice cream. My father, looking even sicker than he had at the beginning of the meal, excused himself and retreated to bed. Evan gave me a sly smile I couldn't interpret.

After finishing dinner and cleaning up, I spirited Gracie to the basement under the pretext of reading to her from the cat book. What I wound up doing was reading her the Riot Act.

"How did Carvel get upstairs?" I asked her.

"She was?"

"Yeah, I had to grab her and take her back down here."

"Well, she can't climb the stairs," Gracie said evasively.

"That's what I thought, but she must have," I said.

"She might have come out of my room," Gracie said, embarrassed.

"Did you take her to your room, you dummy?" I said.

"Don't call me names," Gracie said defensively.

"I'd call you pretty dumb," I said.

"You told me to," Gracie insisted.

"I did?"

"Yes, you said Mommy could hear us down here, so I took Carvel to my room so she couldn't. Hear, I mean," Gracie said. "Did I do something wrong?"

"You can't keep the kitten in your room because Mom is sure to find her. And that's final," I said.

Carvel limped out of the broiler, climbed Mt. Gracie, and sat contentedly on her shoulder. They nuzzled each other like turtledoves as I watched, shaking my head. Then it hit me. I had just made a terrible tactical error. I was going to have to break up Carveleo and Graciet soon, I thought, or poor Dad was going to keel over from his allergies. What better way to stop this nonsense than to have Mom find the lovey-doves in Gracie's room? But I was so wrapped up in the game of Hide the Cat, I had forgotten this was no real contest. I had been on the losing side from the beginning and there was no winning this game—no matter how devious or brilliant I was. All I could do was stall and wait for the inevitable. And I didn't really want to do that anymore.

I grabbed Carvel from Gracie's shoulder and held the little orange kitten in my hand. She didn't wriggle or protest. She just lay there looking up at me. That was a first, I thought, inspecting her burns and sores. They were healing, but Carvel seemed listless and uninterested in what was going on. For the past few days, she had twisted like a tornado and had tried to sink her fangs into me—in a playful way. I didn't have time to reflect on her condition because the blanket to Gracie's fort suddenly flew open.

We're sunk, I thought.

"A kitten. I knew I saw a kitten," Evan said.

I was sitting there like an idiot, Carvel in my hand, but Gracie leaped up, burst into tears, and began begging Evan not to tell. First she pleaded, then she implored, then she sank to her knees in grief and sobbed. Her performance would have made Bette Davis jealous, but it was an unnecessary effort. Evan was delighted with the kitten and enthusiastic about the conspiracy. He was just mad we hadn't told him earlier. While Gracie was wiping her tears and getting out of character, I told Evan about our adventures.

"You mean you've had her here all this time and nobody found out?" he said, amazed. "You guys are good. I can't even hide a comic book in my room. Mom can smell 'em."

Evan liked to read horror comics that my mother thought were inappropriate for him. So he kept most of his stash in my room where Mom never disturbed them. I guess she thought I was old enough for ghouls, cannibals, and flesh-eating zombies. I read them all, of course, but I couldn't say I was a fanatic like Evan.

"How can you waste your money on that garbage?" my mother would ask me with some regularity. "Why don't you read something good?"

I would just shrug. After all, it was Evan's money that went into blood, gore, and mayhem. I was just the circulating library.

"We've been lucky so far," I admitted. "But we've got another problem."

"What?"

"Carvel's been eating Mom's plant," I said.

Evan knew immediately which plant I meant because he went outside the fort and looked at it.

"I can fix it so she'll never know," he said. "All I need is a pair of shears."

In addition to being a horror addict, Evan was an enthusiastic gardener. His small plot in the backyard looked like the Garden of Eden compared to Mom's barren dust bowl.

"Great," I said. "But she'll just chew it up again. I think we've got to give her greens to keep her away from the plant."

"Like broccoli?" Gracie asked, making a face.

"Something easier to eat," I said.

"How about the peas we had for dinner?" Evan said.

"Yeah," I said. "Go on a secret mission and find some peas."

"Cool," Evan said and bolted out of the fort.

He came back with a handful of leftover peas and put them in Carvel's empty food bowl. She sniffed them, but she wouldn't eat any. I couldn't blame her. They looked sad, wrinkled, and unappetizing, so I tossed them out and wiped the bowl.

"Maybe she'll like them raw," Evan said. "I'll get some."

And again he was off at the trot. Evan was far more useful than Gracie when it came to running dangerous conspiracy errands.

He returned with a package of frozen Birds Eye peas.

Well, maybe not that useful.

I sent him back to get a can of peas and an opener. He was back in minutes.

"This is all I could find," he said, holding up two silvery cans of La Sueur peas, the small, fancy kind that Mom usually reserved for guests, figuring frozen peas were good enough for the rest of us. For me, peas were like Evan's comic books. I didn't care one way or the other.

"Go ahead, give it a shot," I said, watching Evan open the can and pour out the contents.

Carvel limped around the bowl, eyeing its contents skeptically. She circled closer and closer, pretending she was totally uninterested in what was there. Then, just as I despaired of her ever even sniffing the peas, she suddenly pushed her entire face into the green monster and slurped up all the liquid. She didn't touch the peas, but she drained the juice like it was champagne. Then she licked her chops and meowed.

"She wants some more," I said.

"Pea juice. That's gross," Evan said.

"Ewww," Gracie said.

But we watched with fascination as the kitten polished off another can of pea juice, meticulously avoiding the actual vegetables. When she was finished, Carvel sighed, sat in Gracie's lap, and went to sleep.

"You've got a weird cat there," Evan said.

"Don't call my cat names," Gracie said.

Now that Evan was a part of the team, he went back to being treated like a brother.

"Actually," I said. "This is great. We finally found a way for Carvel to take more fluids. She doesn't drink much water or milk, so if she likes pea juice, who cares? Maybe she'll get better quicker."

And she better hurry up, I thought, before she's shipped off to an animal shelter. I was all for Carvel, she was a nice little cat and Gracie was wild about her, but when I had seen my father that evening, ready for an early grave, I knew the game was over. The thought of Gracie's titanic fit when I finally gave Carvel up, however, made me uneasy and unable to act decisively.

I was on my way to bed when I heard my parents talking in the living room. I stopped to listen. Good intelligence is always important, sometimes crucial.

"If I didn't know better, I'd swear there was a cat in the house," my father said in a hoarse, strained voice. "This always happens when there's one of those damn things around."

"That's ridiculous," my mother said.

"Then I have to accept the other possibility," my father said sadly. "I must be allergic to Gracie."

"That's even more ridiculous," my mother said. "You can't be allergic to your own daughter. And even if you were, the symptoms would have shown up years ago, not in the last few days."

"I was just thinking that I'll never be able to hold my little girl in my arms again or play with her or kiss her good-night," he said in a tortured whisper.

"I refuse to believe that," my mother said. "Maybe it's her shampoo or her soap or the detergent I wash her clothes in that's causing the problem."

"Have you switched any of those brands?" he asked.

"No."

"Well, there you are. Every time I go near Gracie, my head practically explodes. I can almost feel whatever it is radiate off her in waves," my father said. "I always feel better at work during the day, but when I come home, Gracie climbs all over me and I get worse."

"Maybe she's playing in something she shouldn't. She's been smelling pretty rank lately," my mother said.

"Do you think so?" my father asked hopefully.

"That must be it," my mother said.

But there was no conviction in her voice.

What had I started? I wondered guiltily. I had to let the cat out of the bag. But I was tired and it could wait until tomorrow.

CHAPTER 11

A fter breakfast the next morning, I went outside to get the mail. There, amid the bills and Christmas cards, was something I had been waiting for—a postcard from Diane. Greedily, I savored the picture of a sun-washed beach, sparkling white sand, and impossibly blue water. On the flip side was a message from the woman I loved. It read:

> *The beach is sooo beautiful here and the weather is wonderful! I went water-skiing yesterday and it was a lot of fun. Tomorrow we are going on a tour of the island and that should be fun, too.*
> *Diane*

She had signed it with a little heart to dot the *i* in Diane, but other than that, the postcard was so impersonal that it could have been sent to her Aunt Thelma in Cleveland. Where were the "I love you"s and "Miss you"s and "Wish you were here"s? Was I overlooking some secret message? While I read and reread the card as if it were a scroll from the Dead Sea, Gracie skipped into the kitchen and demanded to know what I was doing. I told her.

"Read it to me," Gracie said.

"You read it," I said. "There's nothing personal in it."

So uncomplicated was the message, Gracie managed to get through it without stumbling over any of the simple, stupid words. Then she asked me if I wanted to play with the kitten.

"Not now," I said. "You go ahead."

That Saturday morning, a week after the advent of Carvel, I was more worried about my phantom love life than the little kitten. All thoughts of saving my father from a slow death by allergy had also evaporated from my head, replaced by disturbing visions of Diane rubbing suntan lotion on her new boyfriend in Jamaica. I was so jealous, so angry, and so confused, I didn't know what to do—except feel sorry for myself.

However, the rude shock of Diane's innocuous words helped me make up my mind about Sally Preston's party that afternoon. My original plan had been to boycott the event for two reasons. First, I felt bad about going without Diane. Somehow, I had it in my head that if I enjoyed myself, I was being disloyal to my official, if distant, girl-friend. That attitude was ruining my social life, but with monk-like resolve, I endured the solitude and boredom of attending only about 90 percent of the parties I had been invited to that season.

Second, I had known Sally since we were in kindergarten and I had always liked her. That made me feel worse. With my highly developed interpersonal skills, I could tell she was interested in me. Also, I had it on good authority that she had told the sister of a friend of a friend of mine's brother that she kind of liked me. She was practically throwing herself at me, I thought. How obvious could she get?

In my limited experience in dealing with girls, I had noted that they didn't want to have anything to do with you unless you already had someone. A guy without a girlfriend had to work his tail off to get one. Lord knows I had. Then, once he was in, all the other girls—magically—decided he was worth dating. It was as if he had received the official Girlfriend Seal of Approval and had suddenly become fair game.

I had almost decided to make a play for Sally and ask her out when a massive infusion of guilt surged through me. What if I were reading more into the postcard than was really there? What if Diane still liked me, but she didn't want to say so for all the world to see? I puzzled over these new thoughts and reached a brilliant teenage solution: I would go to the party, but I wouldn't talk to Sally. The logic was perfect. If Diane still liked me, I was not doing much damage to our relationship. If she hated me, I could always call Sally later to tell her how much I had enjoyed the party—the perfect excuse for picking up the phone.

Bursting with satisfaction at the sharpness of my brain, I was about to visit Carvel in the basement when my mother intercepted me.

"May I talk to you for a minute?" she asked, showing more formality than I was used to.

"Sure."

"I have no right to ask, but Miss Langley just called," she began.

"No!" I said. "I'm not dying for the Wicked Witch of the West. I've got to stay alive for the party."

"At Sally's?" my mother asked. "I thought you decided not to go."

"Yeah," I mumbled.

"That's nice," my mother said. "You should get out more often."

"I get out all the time, Mom, but the only place I ever go is Old Lady Langley's."

"Sally's such a lovely girl," my mother said, skirting the issue.

"I'm glad you approve, but I'm not going to Langley's," I said.

"I know," my mother said, shaking her head sadly. "I suppose I'll have to go myself."

"Be sure to wear high heels—they'll give you good traction on the roof," I said.

"Oh, it's not the antenna. Her tree lights went out again and I'm sure I can change one of those fuse-thingys," she said, without much confidence.

"Just look for the fuse-thingy box in the basement, Mom," I said. "Number five controls the outside lights."

"Oh, Jack, you know exactly what to do and how to do it," she said, buttering me up. "It would take you five minutes and Christmas is only three days away."

"You ought to be done by then, Mom," I said.

Seeing that her ploy was not working, my mother switched her plan of attack.

"I'll try it," she said with a false enthusiasm. "If I fail, I can always get your father out of bed—sick as he is—to help me. You just go ahead and have a good time. Don't worry about us."

The correct answer to that blatantly obvious attempt at emotional blackmail was: "I won't." But I had the steely constitution of a jellyfish and sullenly agreed that I would spend five minutes over there—no longer. If the damn lights didn't go on, I was off. At least my chances of dying in Miss Langley's spider-infested basement were less than buying it on her icy roof.

Thinking about Mom in high heels and a fur coat stomping around Miss Langley's roof made me laugh despite my foul mood. I found it equally hilarious to picture her negotiating the basement trying to figure out how those mysterious fuse-thingys worked. But the thought that she might actually drag my poor father out of bed—the bed that Gracie and I had put him in—had made me give up and give in. I owed him that much.

Resigned to my indentured servitude, I stopped in the basement to grab a fuse. I had noted the last time I was there that Miss Langley had no spares and she was not the sort of person who would think to buy more.

I clumped down the stairs and found Gracie scurrying around on all fours, looking for something.

"What are you doing?" I asked.

"Carvel's gone again," Gracie said, not looking up. "I've got to find her."

"You didn't take her to your room again, did you?" I asked, my stomach sinking.

"No," she said, crawling under the old furniture like a mole.

"You keep looking," I said. "I'll be back in a few minutes to help you."

※ ⚓ ※

I checked my watch to make sure I devoted only a minimum amount of time to Miss Langley's electrical problems and heaved open the bulkhead doors, which the old lady had thoughtfully unlocked for me. The spiders had apparently found new quarters because none of them rushed out to greet me. That was fine, but I could smell mice. I hoped they, too, had the good sense to leave me alone.

As I wrenched open the fuse box, I spotted the brown leather medical bag with a red cross painted on the side. Curiosity overcame my strict schedule and I bent down to open it up. Inside was a bundle of letters bound with a faded red ribbon. The letters was yellow and stiff, indicating that they were old, real old.

I held the bundle up to the weak light from above and found that the one on top was postmarked March 4, 1918. It was addressed in a flowing script to Nurse Frances Langley, San Vitale Hospital, San Vitale, Italy.

Old Lady Langley had been a nurse? I had always assumed that she was a professional nutcase who had been born that way and had been carping, crabbing, and complaining since the age of two. That she had actually held a job amazed me. Even more incredible, Miss Langley had a first name. Had anyone ever called her Fran? I wondered. That sounded too informal for anyone, including her parents.

Intrigued, I carefully slipped a letter out of the envelope and read it.

> *My Dearest Fran,*
> *Every day is torture without you. I think of you,*
> *my dear, every waking moment and you occupy*
> *my dreams at night. I cannot wait until we meet*
> *again on the twenty-fourth, but time seems to pass*
> *so slowly. Oh, if only I could speed the sun's course!*

Pretty corny, I thought, carefully restoring the letter to its envelope. But I realized that there was more to this nasty old lady than I had ever guessed. She had had a career and a boyfriend who claimed to have loved her. He even had the nerve to call her Fran. The thought of anybody even *liking* Old Lady Langley, let alone *loving* her, was astounding.

I pulled another letter from the bundle, this one from the back. It was dated June 10, 1918.

> *My Dearest Fran,*
> *The waiting is almost over, my love, for soon we*
> *shall be man and wife. Oh, how I have dreamed*
> *of that day and how happy we will be. I can pic-*
> *ture us in our own little world where nothing will*
> *matter but our feelings for each other.*

It went on for two pages like that, getting mushier and mushier, and making me embarrassed to read more. I felt as if I were intruding on their privacy—and I was. So I put the love letters back in the medical bag, wondering what had happened to the guy who had written them. He had never married Old Lady...Fran. What had gone wrong? And what was Nurse Langley doing in Italy in 1918?

I filed those questions away and changed the fuse. Then, just as I was leaving, I tripped over a green-painted oxygen container, one of several lined up against the wall. It made a loud clanging noise that instantly brought Miss Langley to the top of the stairs.

"Aren't you through yet?" she screeched at me.

"Just going," I said.

When she disappeared, I bent down to pick up the oxygen canister and found a booklet titled *Living with Emphysema* wedged behind the cylinder. Even with my vast knowledge of tenth grade biology, I had never heard of it, but I assumed that wasn't good and that it required oxygen. I shoved the booklet in my pocket and left the basement.

Outside, the tree lights were as cold and dark as the winter day. I plinked a few bulbs at random, but I was not rewarded with a flash of color. Frustrated, I looked at my watch and found that I had already wasted twelve minutes on this nonsense. My first reaction was to stomp off, but then I remembered two things. First, and most important, I knew in my heart that I was an electrical prodigy and I should be able to get a few strands of simple Christmas lights to work. And second, to my discomfort, I was beginning to see Miss Langley as a real person, not a cardboard crone. That was an unsettling thought, but I decided to give it three more minutes before I gave up.

Using all of my vast electrical engineering knowledge, I kicked the switch box as hard as I could. Nothing. I kicked again, even harder, and this time the lights suddenly blazed forth in a dazzling display of my genius. I limped away from Old Lady's Langley's with a lot to think about.

CHAPTER 12

Figuring that Gracie had already found the missing Carvel, I went to my room to read up on emphysema. I soon discovered it was a chronic lung disease that was incurable. The symptoms could be eased with antibiotics and, for some patients, oxygen. Miss Langley must have it, I thought, and that might explain her irritable behavior— either that or losing her boyfriend forty-four years ago had turned her sour. I thought immediately about Diane. What if she dumped me and I never found anyone else for the rest of my life? Would I wind up like the pathetic Miss Langley? I didn't have time to work myself into a self-pitying funk because Gracie came bursting into my room and told me breathlessly that she had found Carvel, but that the kitten was sick.

"She keeps falling, Jack, and she threw up," Gracie whispered urgently. "You got to come help her."

"Let me get my vet's bag," I sighed.

I followed Gracie down the basement stairs and found Carvel lying on her back, panting. She didn't move when I stroked her head, but she stared at me blankly, blinking her eyes rapidly. Her fur felt damp, as if she had been sweating, which I knew was impossible. When I sniffed her, she reeked of...something.

"Where did you find her?" I asked Gracie.

"Over there, in the wall," she said.

I followed her pointing finger, but I couldn't see anything.

"In the wall?"

"There's a hole behind the old bookcase," she said.

I lugged the scarred wooden bookcase out of the way and saw a jagged hole in the concrete. Protruding from the empty space was a bottle of wine lying on its side. A pool of pink liquid surrounded the open mouth of the bottle. The screw cap lay some distance away.

I picked it up and found that the label said it was a rosé made in New York State. It smelled like Carvel.

I went back to the kitten and watched her as she struggled to her feet and tried to climb onto Gracie's shoulder. But like me on Miss Langley's roof, she was having a difficult time of it. She kept slipping and sliding off Mt. Gracie.

"See?" Gracie said, alarmed.

"She been drinking wine," I said. "Carvel's drunk."

"Oh no," Gracie said. "What do we do?"

"Just put her in the broiler and let her sleep it off," I said. "She'll be fine in a few hours."

"Was that wine in the bottle?" Gracie asked. "Is it Daddy's?"

"Dad doesn't drink wine unless it comes with a cork," I said. "Murf must have left it."

Murf was a former handyman who had been fired by my father for general incompetence and chronic drunkenness.

"I could live with one or the other," Dad had said. "But not both."

"I didn't like him," Gracie said. "He looked at me funny."

"He was probably trying to focus his eyes like Carvel," I said.

Gracie picked up the kitten and, as she did, I noticed a round red ring, about an inch in diameter, just above her wrist.

"What's that mark?" I asked her.

"Dunno," she said.

"Does it hurt?"

"No."

"Don't scratch it," I said. "Maybe it will go away."

That was my mother's advice regarding strange skin eruptions and sporadic outbreaks of poison oak. Her remedy worked most of the time; if not, she would apply an ocean of calamine lotion to the afflicted area and hope for the best.

"Come on," I said. "Just leave her alone."

"Do you want to play with me?"

"Can't. I'm going to a party," I said.

"Can I go?"

"No. This is a grown-up party," I said, herding Gracie up the stairs.

"Are you going to have ice cream and cake?" she asked.

"Nope. Just anchovies, oysters, and sardines," I said.

"Ewww."

Those were just a few of the foods that could elicit such a response from my little sister. As far as she was concerned, if it didn't involve bread, peanut butter, or jelly, it was "yucky."

I went to the bathroom to shave, something I had been doing off and on since I was thirteen. If I let it go for a few days, my beard became noticeable and made me look "thug-like," according to my mother. I liked that idea tremendously, but in 1962 facial hair, especially on teenage boys, was frowned upon. The coolest kid at our school had grown a pair of Elvis Presley sideburns over summer vacation and had been promptly expelled. He was five years ahead of his time. I was barely keeping up with the present.

After I showered and doused myself liberally with Bay Rum, I donned the official party uniform: blue blazer, khaki pants, blue Brooks Brothers dress shirt, black Bass Weejuns, and white cotton socks. The socks always sent my mother into a dither. According to her, only farmers wore white socks. I couldn't verify that because there wasn't a farmer for fifty miles around. All I knew was that all the other kids wore white socks and if I didn't, I would be different—a horror I couldn't contemplate.

I admired myself extravagantly in the mirror and hoped to get out of the house before my mother saw me. No luck. She was lying in wait.

After the standard sock whine, she lit into me for not wearing a tie.

"Nobody wears ties, Mom," I said.

"Your father always wears a tie," she countered.

"He also wears suits and I'm just in a sport jacket," I

said. "It's different."

"But you look so nice in a tie," she said.

Parents have always complained about the way their children dress, but if my mother could have seen me a few years later in a flowered shirt, shoulder-length hair, full beard, and bell bottoms, I'm sure the sin of going tieless would have been forgiven.

"Bye, Mom," I said. "Bye, Gracie. I'll bring you home some roasted octopus eyeballs."

"Ewww."

＊ ✿ ＊

Sally Preston lived in a rambling white house perched high on a hill not far away. I decided to walk because by the time I got the Dodge warmed up, I could have been there. Besides, I knew Sally's parents were among the more enlightened souls in town. They didn't mind if the kids drank beer and I planned to have a few. My parents would have fainted dead away if they had known.

As I trudged up the steep path to the front door, I went over my strategy: have fun, drink some beers, and not really talk to Sally. The odds were pretty good that I would know everybody there, so it was not as if I would be a wallflower. I just had to restrain myself from getting too personal with the hostess.

"Hi, Jack. Glad you could come," Sally said, opening the door.

She was wearing a light gray cashmere skirt and match-ing sweater that hugged the curves of her body as if it had been painted on. She gave me a dazzling smile, which represented thousands of dollars worth of work by Dr. Hudson, the orthodontist. I knew, because in kindergarten Sally had had buck teeth and in seventh grade she had been weighed down with a ton of braces. But she looked so great now that I immediately poured on the charm.

"Uh," I said. "Hi."

She took my coat and led me into the living room which was filled with people from the age of forty-eight to eighty-four. I looked around wildly, afraid I had stumbled into an old folks party by mistake.

"There's dancing and a keg in the library," Sally informed me, seeing my look of dismay.

"Oh," I said with elegance and style.

"I'll be there in a few minutes," she said. "Have you heard from Diane?"

Who?

"Oh, yeah," I said, willing myself to stop looking at her. "Today."

Sally smiled and went off to answer the door, leaving me standing in a roomful of adults, all of whom I was positive were staring at me—and probably my white socks. I fled to the library and was glad to find no one over the age of eighteen. The carpeting had been rolled up, exposing the parquet floor, and a few couples were dancing to the sounds of the local high school rock'n'roll band. The group was pretty bad, but at least they weren't Frank Sinatra, and, after a few beers, they sounded almost adequate.

I found a bunch of my friends standing by the keg, slurping and talking, laughing and joking. I joined them and soon was engaged in the usual conversation and about how cool it was for Sally's parents to put out a keg.

"Sally sure looks good tonight," Dave Simmons said.

"I wish I had her skin," said his girlfriend, Evelyn.

"I'll go get it for you," Dave said.

"Keep your hands off her skin," Evelyn said possessively, grabbing his arm and whisking him off to the dance floor.

I drew myself a beer, glad that I was not the only one who found Sally to be a knockout, and rethought my decision to not talk to her. After reviewing all the facts, I decided that a little conversation was not only appropriate, but required. After all, it was the polite thing to do. I was drinking her draft beer and chowing down on her sandwiches, so what could a few words harm? The problem was, I had no idea what to say. I racked my brain trying to drum up the appropriate party chatter, but I drew a blank. School? No, that was too dull. Football? No, she probably wasn't a fan. Cars? No, she wouldn't be interested. The only other thing I could think of at that moment was cats. She had two, so maybe I could get her involved in a conversation about them.

Nervous as one of the aforementioned felines, I had another beer and paced the floor until Sally's return. I didn't have to wait long before I saw her making a beeline toward me from across the room. When she was next to me, the band suddenly ended their set and the library fell silent—

just as I blurted out, "What do your cats eat?"

The words blasted out of my mouth with the force and noise of a cannon. I could almost see her head jerk back as if I had shot her. The entire room turned to look at me as if I were a space alien. I felt like one.

"What?" Sally said.

"Cat food?" Dave guessed.

"Nothing," I mumbled.

Sally shook her long brown hair as if to clear head and said, "Your mother just called. She wants you to come home right away."

"Past your bedtime, Jack?" Dave said, laughing.

Evelyn laughed with him, completing my humiliation.

"I'll walk you to the door," Sally said, putting her arm through mine and leading the way.

Her touch was wonderful, both exciting and comfortable at the same time. I walked as slowly as possible to prolong the experience. When we reached the foyer, I mumbled my thanks and prepared to flee, a defeated man. But before I could leave, Sally stood on her tiptoes and kissed me on the cheek. Surprised, I turned my head and suddenly found myself locked lip to lip with the prettiest girl at the party. We lingered there for a minute; then she pulled away.

"Bye," she said, smiling.

＊ 🎄 ＊

I slumped home over the snowy sidewalks, not even caring if my Bass Weejuns got soaked. What could be so important that my mother would embarrass me in front of my friends and cut short the greatest kiss I had had in months? Something was up and I was sure it had to do with my co-cat-conspirators.

All the lights in the house were ablaze and I could see the multicolored tree shimmer through the window. The place looked peaceful, even inviting. But when I opened the front door, I came face to face with a tableau of terror. There, standing in a ragged row was an ashen-faced Gracie, her eyes red from crying; an abashed Evan, staring intently at his shoes; and my mother, with steam coming out of her ears. She was wearing the ruined Playtex Living Glove and in her palm was a soundly sleeping Carvel.

"Well?" she said.

CHAPTER 13

Your sister has ringworm and her cat is drunk," my mother said. "What do you have to say for yourself?"

If I had been tongue-tied with Sally, this was much worse. What could I say? When confronted by such overwhelming evidence, I had four choices: deny, deny, deny, or tell the truth. With my mother waving the sleeping kitten under my nose, I decided I wouldn't be able to convince her that Carvel was merely a blot of mustard, a crumb of cheese, or a fragment of underdone potato, causing her to hallucinate. Nor would she believe that Gracie was resourceful enough to have engineered the plot without my help.

"I was going to tell you," I said lamely.

"When?"

"After Christmas," I said.

"Your poor father will be dead by then," my mother said. "What have you done?"

"Saved a dying kitten and made Gracie happy?" I said.

Putting it that way made me sound almost heroic. I wondered if she would buy it.

"You showed incredibly bad judgment," she said. "We treat you like an adult and we expect adult behavior from you. I guess we were wrong."

"Gracie and Evan helped," I said, hoping to expand the conspiracy and diminish my own prominent role.

"They're little kids," my mother said. "I hold you 100 percent responsible."

"If you're going to yell at me all night, at least let me take my coat off," I said, seeking time to get my story together. I wasn't planning on holding anything back, but there are ways to soften the impact of reality.

I settled down on the couch and tried to appear repentant.

My mother, her initial anger flagging, looked at me and said, "You should have worn a tie."

"I promise I'll wear a tie to the next party I go to—which will be in the year 2000," I said, gearing up for a little offense. "Otherwise, my Mommy will call and tell me to come home."

"Don't change the subject, wise guy," she said. "Go ahead and spill the beans. I want to hear everything—and I mean *everything*."

I took a breath and glanced around. Gracie was hiding behind Evan, having decided, I suppose, that I was too dangerous to be involved with. I didn't blame her. Mom was sitting in a chair cradling the now-snoozing Carvel in the ridiculous yellow glove.

I went into the story, trying to make it as complicated and intense as the wine-dark Greek epic we had read in school. When I got to the part about finding the kitten, Gracie worked up the courage to say in a trembling voice, "I made him do it, Mommy."

"Yeah, I wanted to toss it away," I said, indicating that it was all Gracie's fault.

My mother looked shocked.

"You could have taken her to a veterinarian," she said.

"We did," I said. "To Dr. Lindemann."

"Gus Lindemann? He's expensive. How much did he charge you?" my mother asked.

"It was a freebie," I said. "He said it would usually cost more than a hundred bucks to fix her, but he did the work for free because I told him we were poor."

Well, I told him *I* was poor.

"My God, now the whole town will think we're broke," my mother gasped. "What will I say when I see him again?"

"That you're sending him a check?" Evan suggested.

I smiled, but my mother shot him a look that shut him up faster than the hatch on a diving submarine. His chin sunk into his chest and his eyes bored into the carpet.

"Continue," my mother said.

I took my time and told the story in as convoluted a manner as I could, jumping back and forth, then filling in the gaps in no particular order. When I saw my mother's eyes glaze over, I knew my strategy was working. After I had wrung out every possible word, I stopped abruptly, waiting for Mom's reaction.

"Well, it all makes sense now," she said.

It did?

"Gracie's not wanting any presents and her terrible smell," she continued, holding up the tin of salve in her left hand. "And most of all, your father's allergy. How could you let him suffer like that?"

"I'm sorry, Mommy," Gracie wailed. "I didn't mean for Daddy to get sick."

"Jack should have known," my mother said, plunging the guilt knife deep into my back.

The kitten took that moment to open her eyes, stretch, and yawn.

"Can I hold her, Mommy?" Gracie asked.

"No, you'll make your ringworm worse," my mother said. "Nobody's allowed to touch the kitten without gloves."

"What's ringworm?" Evan asked.

"It's a rash," my mother said. "I had it twice when I was a girl. You get it from playing with wild cats."

"Is it serious?" I asked.

"You can't die from it, if that's what you mean," she said. "It's a fungus or a bacterium or something."

"How did you get it?" I asked my mother, wanting desperately to get her going on another subject.

"My sister and I always had cats," she said. "We didn't buy them—nobody ever bought cats in those days. We just put a bowl of milk on the porch and watched as a herd of them came for a free meal. When we found one we liked— my favorite was Blackie—we brought him inside and shooed the others away. After a few days, the cat would be ours and wouldn't run off because he knew he would be fed. Unfortunately, some of them had ringworm and your Aunt Alice and I got it. I don't remember the treatment, but calamine lotion will do for now. I'll see if I can find Dr.

Alexander tomorrow—even if it's Christmas Eve. How about you, Jack, do you have it?"

"Ringworm free," I said.

"Tell me about Blackie again, Mommy," Gracie said, knowing Mom was on a roll and wanting to keep her rolling.

"That was the smartest cat I ever knew," Mom said, smiling for the first time. "He would wake me up for school every weekday morning by jumping up on my bed, meowing, and licking my face. But on the weekends, he would let me sleep in. How he recognized the days of the week, I don't know, but he never made a mistake."

While she was remembering cats past, I noticed that my mother was unconsciously stroking Carvel with her bare hand, risking ringworm and, worse, losing the ire she had been working on since the discovery of the kitten.

That reminded me.

"How did you find out about Carvel?" I asked.

"I went to the basement to water my plant," she said. "And I heard a noise in Gracie's fort. I thought that was odd, but I was more concerned that my last living plant was giving up the ghost and joining all the others in vegetable Valhalla.

"Then, I lit a cigarette and all of a sudden I heard this screeching and the kitten came lurching out of the fort, crying like I had lit *her* on fire. She stopped when she saw me and tried to turn around, but she just fell over—and burped. I couldn't believe what I was seeing, but I found the bottle of wine and figured she had gotten into it.

Imagine, a drunken kitten. Whoever heard of such a thing? The ASPCA would throw us all in the hoosgow."

"Hoosgow?" Evan asked.

"Jail," she said. "You don't watch enough Westerns on TV."

"I do too," Evan protested.

"Well, pay attention."

Suddenly, I realized she was teasing Evan and that floored me. What had begun as an Annihilate Jack session had broken down into a silly nostalgia fest. Perhaps this was the right moment to find out about Carvel's future.

"What are you going to do with her? She's so little and so sick. And it *is* Christmas," I said, blatantly appealing to my mother's holiday spirit.

"We can't keep her," Mom said, continuing to stroke the kitten's tattered orange fur. "With your father's allergy, it's just impossible. Maybe we can find her a good home or take her to a shelter."

"They'll gas her," I said.

"Gas her?" Evan asked.

"Yeah, they keep 'em for a week at the shelter. Then, if they don't find 'em a home, they croak 'em," I said.

Evan turned pale, Gracie burst into tears, and my mother gave me a look that sliced through me like one of Carvel's fangs. I had blown it, I realized. Everything had been going calmly and now I had let the cat out of the bag—Carvel was a goner, dead, kaput, washed up, no more.

Gracie deserted Evan's side and rushed toward my mother,

blubbering incoherently, the tears flowing down her round cheeks. Watching her tortured face, I wished fervently that I hadn't blurted out the truth.

"I'm just kidding," I said with as much conviction as I could muster.

But Gracie wasn't buying it. She was draped over my mother's lap, her arms wrapped around the kitten, and sobbing, "Mommy, Mommy, Mommy."

Although my mother pretended to be strict with Gracie, she was as much of a marshmallow as the rest of us. She transferred her free hand from Carvel's fur to Gracie's hair, no doubt giving her ringworm of the scalp, and made soothing mother sounds, all the while glaring at me as if I were Public Enemy Number One.

While I was cringing on the couch, my father returned from a last-minute shopping trip.

"Ho, ho, ho, *achoo*," he said, sounding like a reindeer-allergic Santa Claus.

Gracie leaped to her feet and flung herself at him, almost bowling the poor man over. The packages he had been holding exploded from his grip and flew around the room.

"Daddy, don't kill my kitty," she sobbed as my father fought to regain his balance. "Please don't kill her. I love her."

My father got down on one knee and wrapped his arms around Gracie, trying to comfort her. At the same time, he looked to my mother for guidance because he had no idea what any of this was about. Then he spotted the kitten and raised his forefingers behind Gracie to make the sign of the cross, hoping, I suppose, to ward off the cat. That sort of thing might work with vampires, but not with Carvel. She jumped from my mother's grasp, hit the carpet with her good leg, and went into a roll. Then she picked herself up, limped over to Gracie, climbed her back, and continued her journey until she settled on my father's shoulder. Carvel meowed and rubbed his face with hers.

I didn't know that cats could sigh, but that's what Carvel did as she adjusted herself on my father's shoulder. Dad didn't sigh, but his face turned lavender, then violet, then burgundy. His eyes closed to slits and I could see the explosion coming from across the room. With a ragged inhale, he coughed with such force that the tinsel on the tree shimmied like a hula dancer's grass skirt. Carvel screeched and arched her back like a Halloween cat, but managed to keep her claws dug into my father's shoulder. Gracie fell on her butt, so surprised she stopped crying.

That went well, I thought.

My father staggered to his feet and grabbed the wall to hold himself up. The next thing he saw was my mother rushing toward him, the rubber glove thrust ahead of her like a yellow lance. Perhaps thinking he was going to get punched, my father ducked, but Mom had pretty good reflexes for an old person and she plucked the kitten off his shoulder, hardly tearing his overcoat.

"What the hell is going on here?" my father finally gasped, no doubt waiting for the next assault.

With his back to the wall, he looked like an escaping

prisoner pinned by the searchlight. Frankly, I wouldn't have blamed him if he walked out the door and never returned, but my father was made of sterner stuff. He poured himself four fingers of cognac and sat at the dining room table, as far away from the rest of us as possible, coughing, sneezing, and gulping his drink.

"Jack?" my mother prompted.

I gave my father the *Reader's Digest* version of the Carvel saga, trying my best to make it seem ordinary and unremarkable. While I was droning to a close, Gracie saved me from having to create a finale by ripping herself from my mother's grip and running into her Daddy's lap. My father began to change color again, this time a lurid shade of plum.

"Don't let Mommy kill my kitty," she pleaded.

"Don't make me the bad guy," my mother said. "Look what you're doing to your father."

Gracie turned on the waterworks, but whether she was crying for her kitten or her father's condition, I don't know. Poor Dad, his eyes puffed almost shut, his nose running, his chest heaving, said, "I lub you. Please go away now."

Gracie cried all the harder, but she climbed down from his lap and ran to her room, leaving all of us staring dumbly after her.

"What are we going to do?" my mother asked, breaking the sudden silence.

"I'll move," my father said.

I don't think he was kidding.

"If you can stand it, let her keep the kitten until after

Christmas," I said. "Then you can kill it."

"Jack!" my mother said. "We'll find her a home."

My father nodded numbly, agreeing to a short reprieve.

"Just keep both of them away from me, so I can die in peace," he said. "Ho, ho, ho."

"Thanks, Dad," I said.

"The one good thing about all of this will be the gift baskets," my father said.

"What baskets?" my mother asked.

"When the neighbors find out we're too poor to feed a cat, they'll probably leave care packages on the front porch. I'm looking forward to the champagne, caviar, pâté, and smoked salmon."

I laughed. We had almost put him in the hospital and he was making jokes. That was a good sign. I took my father aside and told him again how sorry I was.

"I didn't mean to put you through this," I said. "But when Gracie looks at me with those big eyes, I can't help myself. I hate it when she cries."

"Well, I wish you had confessed earlier," my father said. "Then at least I would have known what was wrong with me. But I know what you mean about Gracie. I probably would have done the same thing."

Once again, my father had proved to be a far better person than I was.

I would have killed me.

Part III

December 24–25, 1962

CHAPTER 14

The kitten could feel the darkness sweeping over her, dulling her senses and making her slow and listless. She knew the supply of food might suddenly stop, but no matter how hard she tried, she just couldn't eat anything. The tangy water with the little green pellets in it no longer tasted good to her but made her feel sicker. Even the ragged plant growing in the basement had lost its allure and she couldn't remember why she had found the leaves so delicious only a few days before.

When the little one came to play with her now, she cringed. Their games were just too rough. The feel of hands on her fur made her anxious and uncomfortable. She didn't want to be touched or stroked or kissed. All she really wanted to do was to close her eyes and sleep.

But even sleep was difficult for her because her chest felt heavy and full. It was as if there was a crushing weight on her that prevented her from breathing properly. She found that if she concentrated, she could suck in enough air to make her feel better, but that only lasted a short while and then the darkness would return.

Once, she had licked up some foul-tasting pink liquid and that had made her dizzy. She didn't remember much of what happened after that, but she awoke being held by a stranger. She had tried to get away, but she was being gripped tightly by a yellow rubbery thing. Although she had tried to get away, she had felt the darkness descend and she had surrendered to sleep.

When she had awakened, something had caught her attention. It was big and green and covered with shimmering lights and dangling strips of silver that demanded she bat them with her paws. She had squirmed and twisted, but the yellow glove held her like a vise.

Then another stranger had come bursting into the room and had scared her. With a supreme effort, she had torn herself away from the confining glove, jumped to the floor, and rolled over. Confused getting up, she had run the wrong way and, before she knew it, she was on the shoulder of this new stranger. He had made a loud noise with his mouth that had scared her even more, but within seconds, she had been captured by the yellow glove.

After that, they had left her alone in her hiding place and she was content to sleep and dream of the green, shining thing she had seen. As sick as she was, she knew she had to investigate it, to smell it, to chew it. But every time she tried to get up, the darkness dragged her back down again

Sometime during the night, she had been awakened by her pounding heart and it had taken her a second to realize she couldn't breathe at all. She had shaken her frail body with all her might, but nothing had happened. Then she had drawn a ragged, excruciating breath that had made her see bright colors exploding around her. She had coughed so hard it hurt her chest, but soon the breathing came easier.

The kitten knew there was something terribly wrong with her. She tried to fight it, but she was weak, tired, and losing her will to resist. Somewhere deep inside, she knew that if she just gave in to the darkness, she would sleep peacefully forever.

CHAPTER 15

On Christmas Eve morning there arose such a clatter, I leaped out of bed to see what was the matter. All the stockings were hung by the chimney with care, in the hopes that St. Nicholas soon would be there. Unfortunately, Gracie and Carvel had beaten him to it.

According to the disjointed story I got from her later, Gracie had brought the kitten up from the basement because she thought Carvel might be cold. That was an outright invention, so I cannot vouch for truth of the rest of her tale. However, she said that she had gotten as far as the living room when the kitten had jumped out of her arms and had run full tilt at the Christmas tree. Gracie chased her down and managed to corner the cat somewhere on the middle branches of the tree. But when she tried to retrieve the kitten, she had stumbled over a present and fallen into the tree, knocking it over.

When I arrived on the scene, the tree was lying on the floor. Broken ornaments, pieces of tree lights, and Styrofoam balls were strewn about with abandon. Large glass orbs were smashed to bits, little golden shepherds were decapitated, and Santa Claus was swimming for his life in a pool of sticky sugar water that had spilled from the tree stand. The beige carpet nearby, unprepared for Noah's flood, had turned a muddy brown and, in the midst of the carnage, Carvel, partially hidden by strands of silvery tinsel, squeaked at me. She was lying on the angel that had once topped the tree, alternately licking its face and struggling to free herself from the tenacious tinsel. Gracie was sitting on the floor trying to grasp the trouble she was in.

"Are you all right?" I asked her.

"Mommy's going to spank me," she said.

"And you deserve it," I said. "She told you to keep the cat in the basement, but you never listen, do you?"

"It's all Carvel's fault," she said. "She made me do it."

"Get a better defense," I said. "Look, you broke Mom's angel."

Carvel let out a pitiful meow and I disentangled her from her silvery bonds. Grateful for her rescue, she nipped my finger. I was still holding her when the rest of the family appeared to see the cause of the clatter. They gathered around the tree like mourners at a funeral. After a suitable moment of silence for their fallen comrade, my mother said, "Jack?"

"Don't look at me," I said. "Ask Cat Girl and her partner in crime. And take Carvel. I'm going to wash the ringworm off."

I took as long as I could soaping my hands; then I stood in the doorway of the living room and watched four very disturbed people and one unperturbed kitten. My mother was on the couch cradling Carvel, while my father sat across the room cradling his head. He was probably thinking about all the hours he had put into tinseling the tree. Gracie, who was spotted with calamine lotion, had taken up position behind Evan trying to blend into the background like an oddly colored leopard. She used him as a shield while she spun her yarn.

"It wasn't my fault, I was just trying to save Carvel," Gracie said. "She's sick, you know, and being up in a tree isn't good for her and I had to get her down and everything, but I tripped and fell and the tree went *boom* and fell down and Carvel might have been hurt except for Jack untied her."

There was a pause while everyone tried to follow Gracie's explanation. They didn't succeed.

"Do the words *grammar* and *syntax* mean anything to you?" my father asked.

"No, Daddy," Gracie said, smiling sweetly.

"Just checking," my father said, putting his head back in his hands.

"Gracie, I told you to leave the cat in the stove," my mother said. "But you never listen, do you?"

My God, I thought, I'm starting to sound like my mother.

Gracie and her accomplice were banished to the basement and the rest of us spent the next half hour righting the tree and sweeping up the remains of smashed ornaments and shattered lights. My mother made a halfhearted attempt to save the carpet, but after a few minutes she began hinting that a small chair would fit neatly over the stain.

While my father began the laborious task of redraping the tinsel over the squashed limbs of the tree, my mother picked up the fallen angel and, with a dollop of Elmer's glue, attempted to put it back together again. She was no more successful than all the king's horses and all the king's men.

"Drat," she said.

Mom was not in favor of more colorful swear words.

"Give it to me," my father said, taking a break from the tinseling.

He hefted the broken ceramic angel in his hand as if weighing its chances for survival. The odds didn't look good. The ornament was about eight inches high and had been manufactured at the beginning of the twentieth century by an English porcelain company. The figure wore a blue robe, sandals, and a sad, enigmatic smile that indicated, to me at least, that she was not completely happy about having a pine branch shoved up her skirts once a year. One of her white wings had been broken off long ago and her golden halo was more of a golden *C* because, when he was two years old, Evan had taken a bite out of it. The angel was not much to look at, but like the Curse of the Whitleys, she was a part of Mom's Christmas and had to be preserved at all costs—even if she was now broken into several large pieces.

"Duct tape," my father said.

I shouldn't have been surprised. In an era before superglue, duct tape was the bonding material preferred by the entire male population of the country. Houses, cars, boats, trucks, children, and wives were all held together by duct tape at one time or another. It was good for leaky pipes, broken pieces of metal and plastic, recalcitrant wires, and gaping holes in floors. Gunshot wounds could be bandaged with it, and it was rumored to suck the venom out of snake bites. A shortage of the sticky, silvery tape would have caused a national panic.

I went to the basement to fetch the tape and found Gracie giving Carvel airplane rides. She held the kitten in the yellow glove thrust out before her and ran as fast as she could around the room, making sounds that might have been appropriate for a World War I Spad. The kitten looked distinctly uncomfortable and airsick, so I told Gracie to land and disembark her passenger.

"Carvel doesn't look so good," I said, taking the glove and kitten from her.

"She's beautiful," Gracie countered.

"To you, maybe, but she looks sick to me," I said.

Carvel was lying in my hand with all the animation of one of Gracie's stuffed animals. She was breathing raggedly. Her eyes were closed and her ears were pressed flat against her head. With her eyes squeezed shut, the kitten looked as if she was in pain.

"Did she eat or drink anything?" I asked.

"Not even her pea juice," Gracie said. "She must be scared because she knocked over the tree and she's afraid Mommy will spank her."

I was about to say *Mmmm* when I realized that was my mother's expression and I quickly switched gears.

"Or maybe she's still hung over," I said. "Put her in the

stove, give her the blanket, and let her sleep it off. The best thing we can do is leave her alone. No more airplane rides."

"Can I sing to her?" Gracie asked.

"If you do it quietly," I said.

Then I left the basement, tape in hand, listening to the strains of "Twinkle, Twinkle, Little Star."

Upstairs, my father quickly fused the angel together from the inside, so the silver tape didn't show. The result was a bit bulgy and lopsided, but at least all the pieces were joined together.

"That ought to hold it until you can get it repaired professionally. I just hope this is not an omen," my father said.

"Of what?" I asked.

"Of Gracie's performance this evening."

Every year, our church held what was called "The Pageant," a live manger scene featuring carols sung by the choir and readings from the New Testament by the minister. It was held after dark on Christmas Eve on the grounds of the church and was always dramatically lighted and well attended. School kids from age five to sixteen played all the parts: Mary, Joseph, Wise Men, shepherds, angels, donkeys, horses, and camels.

Joseph and the Three Wise Men were chosen for their ability to fit into the costumes assigned to them. But the selection of the Virgin Mary was a much more serious matter. Casting always caused snickers in the high school and generated the usual jokes about the difficulty of finding an actress who possessed the requisite qualities to fill the role.

Regrettably for their parents, the pantomime animals clumping around the manger were always upstaged by the star of the show—a real donkey named Donkey Oatie. He was a veteran of two decades of highly charged performances, could bray on cue, and was the overwhelming favorite of the kids in the audience.

That year, Gracie had been named "alternate manger angel," a title that had thrilled her because she didn't really understand that she was just an understudy who would never go on unless the real angel, like Miss America, was unable or unwilling to fulfill her duties. Mom had spent weeks trying to let her down gently, but Gracie was positive she would soon be hanging by a wire over the manger. Despairing of ever getting through to her, Mom had gone so far as to make her an angel costume, figuring Gracie could always wear it for Halloween.

Then came the call. The little girl who was to be the angel was abandoning the role of a lifetime to visit her grandmother for the holidays. Mom was aghast, but no one was less surprised than my sister. Gracie had always known she would perform and she had even worked up a routine for her character.

"Mooo…wooo…wooo," she wailed at me one day. "Guess what that is."

"I give up," I said.

"That's what angels say."

"I think you've got angels confused with ghosts."

"She's a Holy Ghost," Gracie told me. "And that's how they sound."

"You might want to check that out with your director," I said.

That was more difficult than it sounded because that season there had been a power grab of sorts for the prestigious position of director. Miss Houghton, the high school drama teacher and longtime producer of The Pageant, had suddenly found herself disenchanted with Mrs. Terry, the elementary school drama teacher who had whipped the kids into shape for the past few years. Miss Houghton, who considered herself a peer of Darryl F. Zanuck, had grown tired of their creative differences and had fired Mrs. Terry. Mrs. Terry, who considered herself the Alfred Hitchcock of pageant directors, had some choice words for Miss Houghton and refused to be fired.

That had led to divine intervention in the form of the Rev. Dr. Hunter, the minister of the church. Dr. Hunter was a craggy-faced baritone who could belt out a fiery sermon that persuaded many of the younger members of his congregation that he was not just talking about God, but that he was God himself. Gracie, for one, was convinced she was saying her prayers to Dr. Hunter every night. That was understandable, because at six-foot-six, he did bear a passing resemblance to Charlton Heston and he looked the way God should look according to stained glass windows—minus the long beard. Yet for all his good looks and good intentions, Dr. Hunter found himself hopelessly outclassed and outmatched by two flamboyant and combative impresarios.

Personally, I would have given the job to Mrs. Terry because, unlike Miss Houghton, she didn't call everyone *dahling* or dress in gold lamé for lunch in the school cafeteria. But after much prayer and meditation, Dr. Hunter showed he had the wisdom of Solomon. In fact, he went one better and cleaved The Pageant in two, giving the high school actors and sets to Miss Houghton and the elementary school actors and props to Mrs. Terry. The all-important control of the lighting was to be a collaboration. Dr. H. had wanted peace on Earth, but he had unwittingly unleashed Armageddon.

"It ought to be fun to watch Miss Houghton and Mrs. Terry fight for custody of the Baby Jesus," my father said, returning to his tinseling. "My money's on Terry. She's got a shorter reach, but she's chunkier and has better lungs. Are you going to the Paj tonight, Jack?"

My father always called The Pageant the "Paj," which rhymed with "badge," indicating he didn't take the theatrical event of the season too seriously.

"Gracie would kill me if I didn't," I said.

✳ 🎄 ✳

There were several inches of snow on the ground and it was sleeting hard when I loaded Gracie into the Dodge and drove the short distance to the church. I had volunteered to get her there early because I wanted to make sure the nerds on the audio-visual squad didn't hang her by the neck. I had seen them in action before and was afraid for Gracie's life.

"Oh no," Gracie said when we were nearing our destination.

"What?"

"I forgot my magic wand."

"Angels don't have wands," I said. "You're thinking fairy princesses."

"But their dresses are almost the same. Their wings, too," Gracie said.

I took a quick look at the outfit, which was stuffed in a shopping bag, and I couldn't disagree. In an effort to make the costume do double duty for Halloween, Mom had made it remarkably similar to the garb of Queen Mab. It was made of frilly, pleated white organdy with gold glitter artfully applied. The wings were store-bought and made of real feathers, while Mom had crafted a glittery halo out of a wire hanger and the shiny gold rope usually strung around Christmas trees.

Because it was cold outside, Mom had insisted that Gracie dress in her warmest clothes. So she had dutifully put on a white shirt, a purple sweater, a pair of blue corduroy overalls, green tights, a pink parka, orange mittens, and her red rubber boots. She was ready for arctic weather or a job filling in for the NBC peacock. The angel costume would be a tight fit over all those clothes.

"Mooo…mooo…wooo," Gracie moaned spookily as we pulled into the church parking lot.

"Practicing your Holy Ghost?" I asked.

"Yes. Mrs. Terry said I should be quiet, but Miss Houghton thought it was a good idea," Gracie said.

It was obvious to me that the war was on and Miss Houghton was trying to sabotage Mrs. Terry's elementary school players. My father had been right. This might be fun.

The manger, a shed made of distressed wood and filled with hay bales, was situated at the crest of a grassy hill. The hill was flat on top but sloped down at a forty-five degree angle to the sidewalk about fifty feet below. From its commanding height, the manger looked both majestic and shabby at the same time. When it was lighted, however, it was a riveting sight shining from the darkness. The layer of snow on the grass and the sleet coming from the skies gave the whole scene a haunting quality that seemed to fit right in with Gracie's eerie wails.

"Manger angel! Where's my manger angel?" Mrs. Terry called out.

"Here I am, Mrs. Terry," Gracie said happily, running over to the drama teacher.

Mrs. Terry was about five-five and weighed in at a good one-eighty. Most of her weight was concentrated in her massive and protruding chest, which made her look something like a rolltop desk. She didn't really walk, but glided like a short, overloaded clipper ship.

"Have you got your costume?" Mrs. Terry asked Gracie.

I held up the shopping bag.

"Have you gone to the bathroom?"

"No," Gracie said.

"Then go now," Mrs. Terry said.

"I don't have to," Gracie said.

"Oh, yes you do. You're going to be up in the air for a half hour and you can't come down until The Pageant is over," Mrs. Terry said.

From her decades of elementary school teaching, Mrs. Terry knew what was really important about putting on a show.

"Jack, take her to the bathroom and make sure she goes. Then get her into her costume so I can inspect her," she said.

"Yes, Mrs. Terry," I said, suddenly feeling like I was back in the fourth grade again.

"Camel Number One! Pull up that costume. Your underpants are showing," Mrs. Terry yelled, dismissing us from her immediate attention. We were on our way when we ran into Mrs. Terry's rival director.

"Hi, Miss Houghton," Gracie said. *"Mooo...mooo... wooo."*

"Excellent, *dahling*," Miss Houghton said "Make sure you bring the sound from your diaphragm."

Unlike Mrs. Terry, Miss Houghton was tall and slim with long blonde hair that probably should have been gray. She carried a polished wooden walking stick that was so long that it came to just below her chin in the Margaret Mead fashion.

"What's a diagram, Jack?" Gracie asked as we made our way to the bathrooms.

"Diaphragm," I said. "It's in your stomach, but don't worry about it. And if I were you, I'd just keep my mouth shut and try to look holy."

"You don't know much about angels, Jack," Gracie said.

She had me there.

We returned with Gracie drained and in costume. I had to admit that she looked cute in the frilly white dress, but she was wearing so many clothes underneath that she was in danger of becoming a pint-size Mrs. Terry.

"Do I get to wear lipstick?" Gracie asked excitedly.

"Go ask Mrs. Terry," I said.

While Gracie went to find the harried teacher, I checked on the harness Gracie would wear under her dress. I found it in a cardboard carton. It was made of brown leather, had brass buckles and fittings, and looked as if would squeeze the life out of Gracie. However, dozens of manger angels had survived the ordeal and had lived to tell about it, so I supposed it would be all right. Then I went to look at the winch that would be used to hoist Gracie into position, eight feet off the ground. I gave it a few turns of the crank and found it was functional.

"Hey, don't touch that," a nasal voice said from the darkness.

"Shut up, Larry," I said.

"Oh, it's you, Jack," the head of the A-V squad said.

"Is this thing safe?" I asked him.

"Sure," Larry said. "I mean, I guess."

Larry was in my class and was considered an oddball. A skinny kid with a bad complexion and stringy black hair, he had a passion for audio-visual machines. He could thread a projector and work the stage lights in our auditorium. He had access to tape recorders, which in those days were the size of small suitcases, and when it came to film strips, he was the best. He no doubt went on to found a multi-billion-dollar electronics company, but I didn't like him.

"Listen, Lar," I said. "You drop my little sister and I'll personally punch your spotlights out."

"Gracie's your sister?"

"And don't forget it."

"Don't worry, Jack. She'll be fine," he said quickly.

"She'd better be," I said as menacingly as I could. "I'll hook her up."

"I'm not supposed to—"

"If I kill her, you're off the hook."

"All right," he said grudgingly. "We'll be ready to go in about fifteen minutes."

I walked to the fringes of the set and waited for Gracie to find me. Sally Preston, however, found me first. Dressed in a dark green coat, a matching beret, and a long red and white scarf, she looked like a particularly enticing Christmas present.

"Is everything all right?" she asked me. "Your mother sounded so upset on the phone."

"Yeah," I said. "Everything's okay. If you've got an hour sometime, I'll tell you all about it."

"I'd like that," she said.

I was peering at her face in the gloom, hoping to get another kiss, when Gracie came bounding over to us. She had dark red lipstick smeared from her nose to her chin, making her looks more clownish than angelic.

"Is this your new girlfriend?" she asked, giving me a wide, lipstick-slathered smile. Her teeth were a ghastly shade of red.

"Shut up, Gracie," I said.

"Hi, I'm Sally. That's a great shade for you."

"Thanks. I put it on myself," Gracie said.

"So I noticed," I said. "Sally, this is my little sister, Gracie."

"I'm the manger angel," Gracie said, throwing out her now considerable chest.

"And you look beautiful," Sally said. "But maybe I can help you smooth out your makeup."

"Did Mrs. Terry say it was okay?" I asked.

"Well, not really. She was busy trying to get Eddie Lawson into his sheep costume, so I borrowed a lipstick from Miss Houghton's makeup table and put it on myself," Gracie said, giving us a ghoulish, bloodstained grin.

"Here, let's see what we can do," Sally said, producing a tissue and wiping Gracie's face clean of all but the proper amount of lipstick.

"There, that's better," Sally said.

"Thanks," Gracie said. "I just wish I had my wand. Miss Houghton gets to carry one. Why can't I?"

"No wands," I said firmly. "Or walking sticks."

Sally looked at me.

"Long story," I said. "I'll need another hour sometime."

"Anytime," she said, smiling. "I've got to find my friends. I'll see you later, Jack. Good-bye, Gracie. Break a leg."

"Will I really break my leg like Carvel?" Gracie asked me in a worried voice after Sally had disappeared into the night. "That would hurt."

"Sally didn't really mean it. That's just an expression for good luck, but you'll probably break your head unless I get you harnessed up the right way," I said.

"Larry almost dropped me when we practiced before," Gracie said.

"Why am I not surprised?" I said. "Get out of the costume so we can put the harness on."

While Gracie struggled to deangelize herself, I went to look at the thin but strong wire that had been strung between two columns of the covered walkway behind the manger. The goal was to hook Gracie to the wire while she was standing on the ground. Then by cranking the wire taut, she would slowly rise into the air, ending up almost three feet over the manger. Because she didn't have to move around, it was a simple rigging, controlled by a single winch. Any idiot, including Larry, should have been able to work it.

I strapped Gracie into the leather harness, then put her costume back on over it and hitched her to the wire.

"Ready?" I asked her.

She nodded, her halo bobbing up and down.

I cranked away and Gracie rose into the night like a frilly moth. When the wire had reached its maximum, I slammed the lock down on the winch and she was floating above my head, swaying in the biting wind.

"How's the view up there?" I asked her.

"The manger's got a hole in the roof," Gracie said. "You should fix it for Jesus."

"This is not my week for roofs," I said.

"I don't see Mommy," Gracie said, twisting around on the wire. "Do you think she'll bring Carvel to see me?"

"Nope," I said. "It's too cold for Carvel and she's sick."

"Poor kitty," Gracie said mournfully.

"Is the harness too tight?"

"No. Can I fly now?"

"What do you mean?" I asked.

"I'm flying, I'm flying," Gracie sang out, moving her arms as if she were doing a breast stroke. "I'm Peter Pan and I'm flying."

"Stop that, Gracie," Mrs. Terry called up to her. "You're an angel. Get into the part, dear. Make it your own."

"Okay, Mrs. Terry."

"I want you to stay still and serene. Keep a small smile on your lips—a smile befitting an angel," Mrs. Terry said.

That will be the day, I thought.

Then the teacher rushed off to settle a squabble between the cow and the horse, who were arguing over who got to eat the hay in the manger.

"I don't think Mrs. Terry knows much about angels, either," Gracie called to me.

"Don't go away," I said. "I want to see how you look from down front."

I slid down the slippery hill, stood where the audience would gather, and turned to look at the floating angel. In the dim light, Gracie looked like a small blimp or a large marshmallow hovering above the manger and kicking her red rubber boots against the roof. I made a note not to raise her that high for the performance so the crowd wouldn't be treated to an impromptu tap dance. But I was relieved to see that Gracie looked just like every other angel I had seen over the years. The distance from the manger certainly added to the illusion.

There were, however, certain advantages to where I would be during the performance—behind the manger was essentially backstage. There, I would have a good view of the cast through a series of missing boards that had been designed to make Jesus's birthplace look old and worn. From my position, I would almost be a part of the production.

After I had cranked her down, I got Gracie under the scant shelter of the walkway. Then we watched Larry, Miss Houghton, and Mrs. Terry, who were scurrying around lining up the players, consulting with the minister, and holding talks with the choirmaster. Periodic arm punching contests swept through the actors and choir alike, causing Mrs. Terry to descend on the miscreants like, well, an avenging angel.

At five minutes to seven, Miss Houghton produced a megaphone and shouted to the milling crowd, "Places, everyone. It's showtime!"

There was a stampede of camels, donkeys, cows, sheep, and red-robed choir members as the kids got into position.

When Mrs. Terry walked over to check up on us, Gracie said, "Break a leg!"

"Why, thank you, dear," Mrs. Terry said.

"That's just an expression," Gracie explained. "I didn't really mean it."

CHAPTER 16

At precisely seven P.M., a single blue-white spotlight illuminated the manger from behind. That was Mrs. Terry's trademark special effect, which created an instant, if muted, Star of Bethlehem glow. Simultaneously, the sleet that had been pelting us miraculously stopped falling from the skies. I could see a few stars, ordinary stars, through the clouds.

The choir began its rendition of "O Little Town of Bethlehem," but they didn't get very far when there was an explosion of pure white light from a car-size spotlight that had been secretly wheeled into place by Miss Houghton's A-V crew. In an instant, The Pageant had been transformed into a Hollywood premiere. The members of the choir covered their eyes and stood in dumb amazement.

"Now that's a star, *dahling*," I heard Miss Houghton say.

"Really, Ina, you've ruined the production. Turn it off this instant," Mrs. Terry whispered savagely.

"Not on your life. I'm going to put some pizzaz in this tired old production," Miss Houghton said, waving her walking stick like a conductor's baton, seriously endangering the lives of those around her.

Mrs. Terry then used a familiar barnyard expression not usually associated with elementary school teachers, at least not while they were working.

"Don't use bad words, Mrs. Terry," Gracie said from the darkness. "Dr. Hunter doesn't like it."

Dr. Hunter, however, did like the sound of his own voice, which was rich and full and boomed out over the public address system:

"And it came to pass in those days, that there went out a decree from Caesar Augustus, that all the world should be taxed."

"You ask me, I pay too many taxes," Mrs. Terry grumbled.

Then the spotlights lit up a manger filled with pantomime animals doing their best to stay in character. The camel mooed, the donkey neighed, and Eddie Lawson, one of the sheep, made strangling noises that sounded as if he were being choked to death. They all seemed to be having a fine time.

"Oh, my God," Mrs. Terry said. "Where are Joseph and Mary? They're supposed to be in the manger."

"They're on the way, *dahling*," Miss Houghton said. "I thought it would be much more dramatic for them to enter stage left."

"But Ina, we haven't practiced this," Mrs. Terry said, her voice quavering.

"Improvise, *toujours* improvise," Miss Houghton said. "It keeps the performance fresh."

After much searching with the spotlight, Larry, the A-V guy, finally found the Holy Family. Mary was sitting aboard Donkey Oatie inspecting her fingernails, while Joseph was around front pulling on the donkey's lead with all his might. Miss Houghton didn't know it, but the donkey had been taught to hold still when someone was on his back so his handler could take a picture. He stood patiently twenty feet from the manger waiting for the camera. A well-trained animal, nothing would move him until then, so nothing happened at all. The three principal players were frozen in the spotlight, a *tableau vivant* without much *vie*.

"Come on, you stupid donkey," I heard Joseph say as he pulled and pulled to no avail.

The choir finished singing "O Holy Night" and waited in suspense to see what would happen next.

"Get off and walk," Miss Houghton stage whispered to her star. "Forget the damn jackass."

Dutifully, Mary leaped off the donkey and made a perfect two-point landing like the gymnast she was. Under her blue costume, I could see her red Keds. Then she stomped over to the manger and sat down on a bale of hay, her legs spread, her hands on her knees, as if waiting for her coach to discuss her performance. Joseph gave up, dropped the lead, and followed her like the dutiful husband he was playing.

I didn't think much of Miss Houghton's improvement and I was not alone in my judgement.

"That was really terrible, Ina," Mrs. Terry sneered.

"It had certain technical problems, Louise. But it was fresh," Miss Houghton said.

"Fresh as donkey sh—"

"Mrs. Terry!" Gracie sang out, ever alert for bad words regardless of who used them.

Once everyone was settled in the manger, Dr. Hunter continued his reading:

"And she brought forth her firstborn son, and wrapped him in swaddling clothes, and laid him in a manger; because there was no room for them at the inn."

Mary reached into the cradle and fluffed up the Baby Jesus' pillows. That key part had been played by a doll for the past decade after a terrible experience with a real baby had almost ended The Pageant for all time.

Everyone knew the sordid details. Eight-month-old Peter Benson had been volunteered by his mother to interpret the part of Jesus and Pageant officials had gratefully accepted her offer. But once the show started, Peter began to wail furiously and wouldn't stop. That year's Mary, her maternal instinct taking over, had picked the baby up to comfort him. But once he was in her arms, Peter was immediately seized by a massive bout of diarrhea, soiled his swaddling clothes, and threw up on his Holy Mother. Not being wise to the ways of leaky infants, Mary had dropped the baby into the cradle from a height of about a foot and had shouted "Gross!" at the top of her lungs. Then she walked away from the crying child and out of show business forever.

Mrs. Benson had rushed into the manger to rescue her son, yelled at a stunned Joseph, and gave Miss Houghton the tongue-lashing of her life. It all made for compelling drama, though perhaps not in the spirit of the season.

We waited patiently for the choir to finish singing "Hark! The Herald Angels Sing" and for Dr. Hunter to approach the microphone again.

"And there were in the same country shepherds abiding in the field, keeping watch over their flock by night," the minister intoned.

Larry swung a spotlight to the designated area and caught the shepherds dueling with their crooks in a four-way melee. When the light hit them, they stopped in mid-sword fight and realized they had been caught. The usually astute Mrs. Terry must have forgotten a basic law of nature: give a boy a stick and either he will try to shoot or fence with it.

"Children!" Mrs. Terry shouted and the shepherds calmed down and ambled to center stage, their heads hanging in shame. On the way, one of the repentant ten-year-olds accidentally clipped Donkey Oatie with his crook, which made the poor beast bolt. He loped right into the manger and cowered in a corner, his hindquarters to the audience. Then he noticed the hay and began noisily munching on it.

"My God," Mrs. Terry said.

"Your shepherds were a bit rough," said Miss Houghton with some satisfaction. "But the donkey has star quality."

"And, lo, the angel of the Lord came upon them," Dr. Hunter read with feeling, "and the glory of the Lord shone round about them: and they were sore afraid."

That was Gracie's cue.

"Up we go," I said, cranking the handle of the winch.

"Whee," the alternate angel of the Lord trilled.

When I had her into position, I applied the lock and

Gracie descended gently to the ground.

"Damn thing's busted," I said.

"Get her back up there," Mrs. Terry said, her voice a strangled screech. "Hurry!"

I cranked for all I was worth and soon had Gracie back in the proper position over the manger. Illuminated by the ten-million watt spotlight Miss Houghton had introduced, she looked a bit washed out, but her gold sparkles and halo shone like fire. She raised her arms as if to encompass the Holy Family and beamed beatifically. Never losing her rapturous smile, she said loudly enough for me to hear: "Jack, I have to go to the bathroom."

"Hold it," I said. "Or just go. But you're not coming down until it's over."

"Mooo…mooo…wooo," Gracie said from her diaphragm.

"Gracie, be quiet," Mary said, noticing her for the first time through the hole in the roof.

"I am the manger angel," Gracie said in a robot-like voice. *"Wooo! Wooo!"*

Mary might not have been scared, but the shepherds were spooked. In unison, they hit the ground on their knees, sore afraid indeed.

Pleased with her power over her flock, Gracie began doing an energetic breast stroke in the air, *woo*ing and *moo*ing.

"Stop it," I called to her. "I can't hold you. Just stay still."

"And the angel of the Lord said unto them, fear not: for, behold, I bring you good tidings of great joy, which shall be to all people. For unto you is born this day in the city of David, a Saviour, which is Christ the Lord," Dr. Hunter read.

The shepherds, having recovered from Gracie's sudden appearance, shuffled on their knees to the cradle and looked at the doll worshipfully. Taking their cue from the shepherds, the pantomime animals also crowded around the cradle, jockeying for position to see the baby. Then the eight-year-old boy playing a camel reached out a camel-colored glove and gave the doll a poke in the stomach.

"Mama, Mama," the doll said.

Mary looked surprised.

"Mama, Mama," the doll repeated, over and over again. The camel must have been the straw that had broken the mechanism's back.

Mary scooped up the baby and shook it, but it continued to cry, "Mama, Mama."

"Mary, the baby's crying," Gracie called out helpfully from on high.

Fortunately, the choir burst into a rousing version of "Joy to the World," which masked the noisy commotion in the manger.

"Where is Peter Benson when we need him?" Mrs. Terry said pointedly. She had not been involved in that debacle, but she had witnessed it.

"Just bury it under the pillows," Miss Houghton called out to Mary.

I thought that was disrespectful to the Baby Jesus, but the constant noise was grating on my nerves and, when combined with the strain of holding Gracie up, I suddenly thought that Miss Langley's mouse-infested basement wasn't so bad—or at least it was warm and dry. I wondered if I could catch emphysema by standing around in the cold.

I looked up at Gracie and saw that her wings were askew, the white dress was quickly losing its glitter, and her halo was in danger of falling off. How much longer would this go on? I wondered.

"When they saw the star," Dr. Hunter said into the microphone. Then he put his hand over the mic, squinted at Miss Houghton's industrial-size spotlight, and said, "And how could they miss it?"

The choirmaster, who was standing nearby, laughed.

"When they saw the star," Dr. Hunter said again, "they rejoiced with exceeding great joy. They saw the child with Mary his mother, and fell down, and worshiped him: and when they had opened their treasures, they presented unto him gifts; gold, and frankincense, and myrrh."

"Hey, Mary, the Three Wise Guys are coming," Gracie said, using her lofty vantage point to keep the Holy Family fully informed about arrivals and departures. She held her hand over her eyes like an Indian scout and squinted into the hazy darkness.

Sure enough, the trio of Magi came trooping across the snow-covered lawn, looking splendid in their richly embroidered robes and colorful turbans. These were the high school students with the proper dimensions for the lavish costumes and they were solemn and professional, placing their presents at the foot of the cradle, just as the choir finished "We Three Kings of Orient Are."

After a medley of "Away in a Manger," "O Come All Ye Faithful," and some modern carol I didn't know or approve of, the proceedings came to a close.

"And suddenly there was with the angel a multitude of heavenly host praising God and saying, Glory to God in the highest, and on earth peace, good will toward men. Amen," Dr. Hunter said, finishing with a flourish.

"And I really mean it," he added in sotto voce.

As the choir began singing "Silent Night," Miss Houghton's supernova erupted into an orgy of colors as Larry applied giant gels to the burning spot. The sky exploded into red, yellow, orange, and blue columns of light, a kind of fireworks display that was spectacular, if not particularly appropriate. The night was neither silent nor even night after that. The soggy crowd *ooh*ed and *ahh*ed appropriately, causing Miss Houghton to turn to Mrs. Terry and say, "Ta-dah, *dahling*."

Then everything went black and the skies opened up with a barrage of snowflakes. God's plan to douse the spot- light? I wondered.

"Get me down from here, I'm cold," Gracie called to me.

I released the crank and—nothing happened. When I had let go before, Gracie had come floating to earth in a

gentle glide. Now she was stuck up there. I kicked the mechanism, but it was locked into place.

"Jack!"

"Larry, get over here and help me with this thing," I yelled.

Together, we managed to bring Gracie to within three feet of the ground, but there she stalled and swung to and fro like a puffy white pendulum.

"Get some wire cutters, " I said to Larry.

"I can't be responsible for the destruction of church property," Larry said.

"But you can be responsible for your own life," I said menacingly, advancing on him.

Larry took the gentle hint and disappeared into the church.

"Get me down, Jack," Gracie called piteously.

"In a minute," I told her.

That's when I heard it, a kind of high-pitched banshee wail, getting closer and closer, the volume growing by the second. I went around to the front of the manger and there, in the semi-darkness, I could see a mass of small figures surging up the hill. In the dim light, they looked like sepia pictures I had seen of the Oklahoma land rush. At least fifty children between the ages of three and twelve were struggling to reach the manger and worship at the hoof of their idol, Donkey Oatie. I had forgotten that every year at the conclusion of The Pageant, a contingent of kids always fell upon the poor creature and lavished him with gifts—

apples, sugar, and loving embraces. I had been in their ranks fewer than ten years before, though I would never have admitted that to anyone.

The children were having a difficult time in the slippery snow, so the mass soon broke up into waves of kids separated by age. The older ones were quickly making the ascent, while the little ones were struggling just to stay afoot. One boy, who was stuck about halfway up, suddenly hit the deck and slid back down the hill like an out-of-control toboggan. He was carried off the field by his father, who promised to buy him a damn donkey if he would only stop crying.

The rest of the children mobbed the manger, surrounded Donkey Oatie, and thrust their presents at him with less-than-gentle hands. Although he had vast experience at being the center of attention, the donkey was not having a good night. First, he had been ignominiously sat upon by a large girl who was much heavier than the tiny passengers he usually allowed on his back to take a picture. Then someone had thwacked him with a stick, scaring him half to death. And now he was hemmed in by rowdy children who were smacking him on the shoulders, sides, and back end. All he wanted to do was get out of the confining manger, find his handler, and retire for the night in his warm stall.

With a bray of frustration, Donkey Oatie backed out of the manger, shedding half a dozen clinging parishioners, and trotted away to find his handler. The children followed in hot pursuit. Looking about wildly, the donkey galloped first one way then another, all the time being chased by his adoring posse. In desperation, he ran behind the manger and there he saw something donkeys don't see every day—Gracie's red boots hanging in the air before his eyes. He stopped short, brayed loudly, and a took a nip of red rubber.

"Oww!" Gracie yelled and kicked at his head. "Bad donkey, don't bite."

In suburbia, we were all livestock deprived, so I was dubious about my ability to rescue Gracie's two feet from her four-footed attacker. Donkey Oatie wasn't all that big, but he had a full set of long, yellow choppers that looked as if they could do some real damage. I was spared making a heroic decision by the pack of kids who came running at the donkey with love in their hearts and apples in their hands.

Then began an intricate square dance. On one side was the donkey who, with mincing steps, was trying to avoid the throng of children and bite the vexing boots. On the other side were the kids who do-si-doed in for a fast pet and alamained right for a chance to shove a piece of forbidden fruit into the beast's mouth. Gracie, caught in the middle, looked as if she were riding an imaginary bicycle, trying to keep her toes from becoming donkey chow. She was being bounced around like a waterlogged piñata in a hurricane. Finally, Donkey Oatie decided that the children were more annoying than the boots and took off at full speed, followed by the howling mob.

"That was something," Larry said from his hiding place behind a pillar of the walkway.

"Gimme the wire cutters," I said.

I had Gracie down in a minute and, as I was unharnessing her, Miss Houghton and Mrs. Terry came strolling by.

"A pretty peppy show, eh, Louise?" Miss Houghton said.

"You're insane, Ina. A genius, but insane," Mrs. Terry said.

"Ha!" Miss Houghton said, completely vindicated.

"There's my little manger angel," Mrs. Terry said. "Nice job, Gracie. At least you didn't fall—that's half the battle."

"And your sound effects were marvelous, *dahling*," added Miss Houghton. "You know, Louise, perhaps we should mic next year's angel. All those *mooo*s and *wooo*s would be sensational."

"Give it a rest, Ina," Mrs. Terry said. "I need a drink."

"My thoughts exactly, *dahling*," Miss Houghton said. "You see, we make an excellent team after all."

They walked off into the night congratulating each other on their brilliant avant garde revival of the Christmas story. They hadn't been gone for more than a minute when Gracie said in a scared voice, "Oh, no, here he comes again."

I looked up and saw Donkey Oatie hightailing it toward us at good clip.

"Run into the manger," I told Gracie, while I stood my ground, determined to bring the creature to heel. Waving my arms and shouting "Whoa, boy," I tried to get him to stop, but he veered away from me and trotted directly into the manger.

Figuring I would find Gracie stomped to death or eaten alive, I went around front and witnessed, to my surprise, a scene from "Peaceable Kingdom." Gracie was standing near the recently renovated cradle offering Donkey Oatie a handful of hay and petting him on the head.

"You'd like my kitty, " Gracie was telling the donkey. "Her name is Carvel and she's real small and kinda sick, but she's very nice and she could ride on your back like Mary did and you could be friends. And I could ride you, too."

The donkey didn't have time to respond to Gracie's invitation because his red-faced handler, out of breath from chasing the wayward donkey over hill and vale, grabbed him by the bridle and led him away.

"Bye, Donkey Oatie," Gracie said. "See you next year."

I sat on a hay bale and listened to the doll repeat "Mama, Mama" over and over again, thinking that everyone would remember this particular production for years to come.

"Here comes Daddy," Gracie yelled, running out of the manger and jumping into his arms.

"You were so beautiful, sweetie," he said. "You're my little angel."

"Where's Mommy?" Gracie asked, looking around.

"She's in the car waiting to tell you how wonderful you were," he said. "We especially liked your double entrance."

"I went up. Then I went down," Gracie said. "Then the damn thing broke, right Jack?"

"Gracie!" I said.

"But I didn't break my leg. That's just an expression," Gracie said.

"Thank goodness for that," my father said. "See you later, Jack?"

"Yeah, I'll be home soon."

I was wet and cold and my arm hurt from keeping a death grip on the winch. It wasn't even eight o'clock yet, too early to go home, but too late to find out if any of my friends were around. In those days, Christmas Eve was not a big party night. Parents demanded their children stay at home and most of us did.

I scraped the ice and snow from the windshield of the Dodge and drove slowly through the deserted streets looking for someone I knew. But not a creature was stirring except the snow plow. The driver, raking in triple time, was singing carols loudly and off key.

I was just about to give up when I had an idea. I would drive to Sally Preston's and wish her a Merry Christmas. Buoyed by that thought, I crept over the slippery roads and parked at the base of the hill where she lived. Then it dawned on me that I didn't have a present for her, so I just sat in the cold car and looked at the lights shining brightly from her house. I listened to WMCA on the radio and wished fervently that the Chipmunks had avoided singing Christmas songs. I also wished I had a real life and wasn't a stupid teenager with nothing to do and no place to go except home.

Finally, I accepted my dismal fate and started the car. The wipers made angel-wing patterns in the snow as I resigned myself to long hours of boredom.

CHAPTER 17

I don't know what I was expecting, but when I arrived home I found all the lights out and Evan sitting expectantly by the telephone. The furnace was off and it was cold in the house.

"What are you doing sitting in the dark?" I asked.

"She's gone, Jack," Evan said.

"Who's gone?"

"Gracie, and she took Carvel with her," he said.

"What are you talking about?" I asked. "I've been gone for less than an hour and the whole place goes to hell. Where are Mom and Dad?"

"Out looking for Gracie," he said.

I flipped on some lights, turned up the thermostat, and sat down next to Evan.

"Now," I said. "Tell me what's going on."

"When we came home, Gracie went to check on the kitten. Then she came back upstairs crying and saying that Carvel was real sick and that Mom should come look at her."

"And?"

"Mom brought the cat into the kitchen and, I swear, Jack, the way she was breathing, I thought Carvel was dead. She wheezed and coughed and kinda panted."

"What did Mom do?" I asked.

"She said they had to get Carvel to the animal hospital

right away, but Gracie began screaming and crying. I never saw her so upset and she wasn't pretending."

"Okay, so they were going to the hospital. Why did Gracie run away?" I asked.

"I don't know," Evan said. "She started yelling something about veterans killing her kitten and the next thing I knew, she was gone and so was Carvel."

"I thought Gracie was through running away," I said.

"She used to do it all the time, but back then she wasn't mad or crying or anything," Evan said. "She just liked to go where the cookies were better."

Evan was right. In her wandering days, Gracie had scoured the neighborhood hunting for cookies, Cokes, and conversation. She would barge in on total strangers, introduce herself, and keep the homeowner engaged in idle chatter for as long as the Oreos held out. Then she was off to make new conquests and eat new cookies.

"Did Mom and Dad call the police?" I asked.

"No. They talked about it, but Dad said that Gracie couldn't get far in this weather," Evan said. "Besides, if she went to a neighbor, they would probably have the sense to call. That's why I'm sitting here, but nobody has called yet."

"Do you have any idea where she might be?" I asked.

Evan shook his head.

"We have to think this out logically," I said. "If you were six years old and had a sick kitten, where would you go?"

"To the animal hospital," Evan said.

"She already had that chance and she went nuts," I said.

"No, she'll find somebody to fix her cat."

"Dr. Lindemann?"

"Maybe," I said. "But you said she hates veterans—that's veterinarians."

"I wondered," Evan said.

My giant scientific brain was failing me as I tried to put myself in Gracie's red rubber boots: *I'm scared, I'm tired, but I'm determined to save my kitten. I can't walk very far because it's snowing outside. And although I'm dressed warmly, I'm wet and upset and not thinking very clearly. Where would I go?*

"She's has to be nearby," I said. "You stay here. I'm going to find her."

I hit the streets with a determination that quickly faded under the onslaught of the snow, the wind, and the biting cold. There was absolutely no one out and about on the night before Christmas. Sensible people were drinking eggnog by the fire and were glad of it, I thought.

I shoved my hands deeper into my pockets and hoped that the upturned the collar of my coat would keep the snow from leaking down my neck. A gust of wind almost stopped me in my tracks, making me wonder how long Gracie could stay out in weather like this. A pair of lights appeared at the top of the hill, turning the snow into a swirling mass of individual flakes. Then the plow came over the rise and I could hear the driver singing praises to Good King Wenceslas. He was still off key. The driver, that is.

Trying to avoid the worst of the wind, I ducked down the side street that led to the playground, hoping I wouldn't find

Gracie frozen to death in a snow drift. No little pink parkas were in evidence, but I saw that Miss Langley's lights were blazing away like a beacon. That's when it struck me that Gracie might know that the Old Lady Langley had been a nurse. Put it together, I thought, think like Gracie: nurse, doctor, fix cat. That sounded like a six-year-old's logic, so I pushed on to the front door. Even if this were a dead end, I would have the satisfaction of disturbing Miss Langley on Christmas Eve.

The trees I had strung with lights shone brightly in the night, convincing me that I had a promising career in Christmas decoration if the scientific thing didn't work out.

I rang the bell and waited, hoping Miss Langley didn't have any chores for me to do.

After a minute, Gracie opened the door, looked at me, and slammed it in my face.

"Nice to see you, too," I said to the door.

I rang again and this time Miss Langley flung the door open and stared up at me with a scowl on her face. She was wearing a green bathrobe, pink slippers, and some sort of frilly night cap. Her hearing aid was plugged solidly into her ear.

"How dare you!" she shrilled at me. "I didn't think you'd have the nerve to show up here."

"I came for Gracie," I said.

"Why? So you could torture her some more?"

"What has she been telling you?" I asked, bewildered.

"You leave her all alone on Christmas Eve and then you

come home and want to kill her kitten," Miss Langley said indignantly. "I should call the police. I've never heard of such a thing."

"You've never heard of such a thing because it's not true," I said. "Gracie, come out here and tell the truth."

Gracie sidled out from the living room and stood behind Miss Langley.

"The truth," I said.

"Well, I wasn't really alone," she said in a small voice. "But they were trying to kill my cat with veterans."

Miss Langley made a phlegmy sound that only old people can make and said to me, "You'd better come in, then."

Gracie had been right. The interior of Miss Langley's house looked as if it had been designed using Dr. Lindemann's office as a model. Everything was old, ornate, and covered with fussy doilies. It was dark, cramped, and the air smelled like it had been trapped inside since the nineteenth century. I kept thinking about funeral parlors and looking for caskets in the corner.

We walked down a dim, narrow hallway to the living room, with Gracie leading the way. I sat gingerly on a small chair covered in a frayed silk that might once have been blue, but was now a grayish-brown. The chair creaked alarmingly every time I moved. Miss Langley probably never had visitors who weighed more than a hundred pounds, I thought, looking at the equally spindly sofa. The wallpaper was faded, but giant multicolored blossoms still leaped out at me from a twisted green jungle. The uneven floor was covered with a green Oriental rug that needed a good cleaning.

"Did you or did you not lock this poor child out of the house and make her stand in the snow?" Miss Langley said accusingly.

"Absolutely not," I said.

"Then why is she so wet?"

"Because she just got through being the manger angel at The Pageant," I said.

Miss Langley gave Gracie a disapproving look that would have made me admit to a murder, even if I hadn't done it.

"What are those splotches on your arms?" Miss Langley asked.

"Calamine lotion. I got worms," Gracie said.

"That's ringworm," I said.

"I'm sorry, Miss Langley," Gracie said, her lip trembling. "It's just I didn't know what to do. My cat is sick and they wanted to kill it."

"Is that true?" Miss Langley asked me.

"No," I said. "All we wanted to do was take the kitten to the animal hospital."

"She'll die there," Gracie said, the tears leaking down her cheeks. "Jack can't fix her, the veteran can't fix her, only you can fix her, Miss Langley. Please."

"Look, Miss Langley," I said. "I'll take them home right now and we won't bother you anymore."

"This is not exactly how I envisioned I would spend Christmas Eve," she mused. "But unless someone does something about that cat immediately, it will die. How long will it take you to get to the animal hospital?"

"In the snow? More than an hour," I said. "With no snow tires, maybe longer."

Miss Langley made that phlegmy sound again.

"I'm no expert with animals," she said. "But if this were a person, my diagnosis would be pneumonia."

"But we've been giving her penicillin," I said. "Right, Gracie?"

Silence.

"Gracie?"

"Are those the pills Carvel hates?"

"Yes."

"Well, she didn't like them so I stopped giving them to her."

"Smooth," I said. "Now she's got pneumonia."

Gracie burst into tears, covering her face with her small hands.

I felt terrible. This was all my fault, I thought. Who in his right mind would entrust a six-year-old with such an important task? It was like letting Gracie handle a loaded gun. Sooner or later something bad was bound to happen. I should have known that.

"I'm sorry, Jack," Gracie wailed. "I'm sorry, I'm sorry. I didn't mean to do anything wrong."

"It's all right, Gracie," I said, getting out of my chair and patting her on her damp head. "I should have done it myself."

"Do you have any of it left?" Miss Langley asked.

"The bottle's in the stove," Gracie managed to say.

"Then go get it and we'll see what we can do."

"I've got a better idea," I said. "Let me call home and have my brother bring it over. That way, he can leave a note for my parents."

"Where are they?" Miss Langley demanded. "Why aren't they home?"

"They're looking for Gracie."

"Oh. Phone's in the kitchen," Miss Langley said.

The kitchen was as I expected it to be—old fashioned. The stove and the refrigerator looked like the ones we had thrown out years ago. The white paint on the cabinets was peeling and I noticed that two of the handles were missing. On the floor, the green and white linoleum was worn through to the bare wood in places. If she had wanted to, Miss Langley could have kept me employed for months just making repairs to the kitchen.

I found the black rotary phone on the wall and dialed home. Evan answered on the first ring.

"I found Gracie," I said. "She's at Miss Langley's and she's okay. But I need you to do another secret mission. Lives depend upon it."

Enthusiastically, he agreed. To get Evan to do anything, you had to make a game out of it.

"Get a piece of paper," I told him. "And write the following coded message: M. and D.: Gracie's fine and at Miss Langley's house."

There was a pause while he was writing.

"M. and D. is for Mom and Dad. No. It's L-a-n-g-l-e-y. Right. Now go to the basement and look in the stove. You'll find a bottle of pills. I want you to bring them here as fast as you can. What? To Miss Langley's, dummy. Where else? And remember, someone may die if you fail."

After I had hung up, I went to inspect Miss Langley's infamous and many-times-replaced windows. She had looked down on me from here for years—in both senses—so I thought it was only fair that I saw the world from her vantage point. The rows of small windows gave the snow-covered playground a fragmented appearance, as if I were seeing it through an insect's eye. I couldn't really focus on anything in particular and the complete view was too broken up to be comprehended as a whole. It was obvious to me that Miss Langley saw the world in a completely different way than other people. Her windows must make her cranky, I deduced brilliantly. Then I went back into the living room to wait for my brother.

I must have been dramatic enough to motivate him, because Evan was at the door in ten minutes, penicillin in hand.

"Who's going to die?" he asked breathlessly, shaking the snow from his ski jacket.

"Carvel, maybe," I said.

"Oh," he said, disappointed. "I thought—"

"Can either of you build a box?" Miss Langley said, interrupting.

"I can, " Evan said.

He always thought he could do anything, even if he couldn't. If Miss Langley had asked who was available to split an atom, Evan would have volunteered.

"Then make me a box about *yea* big," Miss Langley said, holding her hands two feet apart, "and four inches high. You'll find a hammer, nails, and some scrap wood in the basement."

Evan suddenly seemed uncomfortable. I had told him all about the mice and spiders down there, so I suppose he was having second thoughts about going to the basement alone.

"I'll help you," I said.

"Thanks, Jack," he said gratefully.

We found the hammer, some rusty nails in a torn cardboard container, and an assortment of splintery wooden boards that seemed to be too flimsy to hold a nail. I improvised by breaking down an abandoned milk crate and used the wood to frame the project. It didn't take long to fashion a crude box—even with my brother hovering over my shoulder offering his unsolicited and uninformed advice.

"I don't know what she plans to do with this," I said, holding up the finished box. "But let's get it upstairs before the mice come out to play and bring the spiders with them."

Evan bolted for the stairs, while I laughed. Then I saw a blur of brown fur out of the corner of my eye and realized that my prediction had come true. All the creatures were stirring, including the mice. I almost beat my brother up the stairs.

We found Gracie and Miss Langley in the kitchen attending to the inert kitten, who was lying on the table. Carvel looked like she was already dead to me, but I kept quiet lest I set Gracie off again.

"Hold him," Miss Langley said to Gracie.

"Her," Gracie said.

Miss Langley opened the cat's mouth and shoved in two pills. After that, she rubbed the cat's throat until she was satisfied both were resting comfortably in Carvel's stomach.

"Too little, too late, probably," she said. "Where's the box?"

"I made it," Evan said proudly, grabbing the box away from me and presenting it to Miss Langley.

"Not a very good job," Miss Langley said. "But I suppose it will have to do."

"Jack made it," Evan said. "Really."

I laughed, but if I had been a few years younger I would have punched him.

Miss Langley put the box on the table and lined it with a tattered pink towel. Then she picked up the kitten and placed her in the middle on the makeshift bed. Carvel never moved; she only breathed raggedly.

"Get some wire hangers out of the hall closet," Miss Langley said.

The tone of her voice made Evan shoot out of the room as if he was in a footrace and wanted to win.

"Jack, go up to my bedroom and get my oxygen bottle. It's next to the bed."

"Yes, Miss Langley," I said meekly.

I walked up the narrow staircase, feeling as if I were entering a haunted house, and felt my way along the hallway in the dark. There were three doors upstairs and, after a moment's hesitation, I chose door number three. Monty Hall would have ridiculed me. There was nothing in that room.

"I'll take door number two," I said aloud.

The door swung open on Miss Langley's bedroom. I had hit the jackpot—unless I could convince Monty to give me the cash instead. I felt for the light switch and turned it on.

The bedroom was not very large, but the bed was enormous. It had a dusty silk canopy hanging over it, making me wonder if a paratrooper had landed there recently. The mattress sagged in the middle and I could see the outline of where Miss Langley slept. The dark wood on the headboard was carved with scenes of fat little cupids embracing each other and cavorting about wildly. Such frantic action would have kept me up all night, but I supposed Miss Langley was used to it. The bed looked a lot older than she was.

I spotted the oxygen canister immediately. It was painted green like the ones in the basement, but this one was only a fraction of the size. Attached to it was a clear plastic mask with rubber straps. Despite its small size, the oxygen bottle was heavy.

When I returned to the kitchen, Miss Langley had bent the wire hangers into three hoops that she was busily securing to the box I had made. When she finished, she had made a kind of frame over the sleeping Carvel.

"Give me the bottle," she said.

When I handed it over, she turned on the valve and I could hear the hiss of oxygen. Then she took the mask and placed the kitten's head and shoulders into it. Carvel didn't resist.

"Her lungs are full of fluid," Miss Langley said. "She's having difficulty breathing and we have to help her the best we can until the penicillin starts working. It's a race against time that we will probably lose. Get me that Saran Wrap on the counter."

Deftly, Miss Langley tore off sheets of the clingy plastic wrap and draped them over the three bent wire hangers lining the box. She smoothed out every piece, being careful to overlap each one. When she was done, she went to a kitchen cabinet and pulled out a roll of duct tape and secured the plastic to the sides of the box. My father would have congratulated her on her choice of tape.

Then she sat back and looked at her creation with a critical eye.

"It's an ersatz oxygen tent that is not very efficient or very well sealed, but it will have to do for now," she said with a sigh.

"Will she be all right?" Gracie asked her.

"I don't know," Miss Langley said. "But you had better

be prepared for the worst."

"What's that?" Gracie asked.

"The kitten could die," Miss Langley said bluntly. "In fact, the odds are she *will* die."

Gracie began sobbing again.

"Everything dies, Gracie," Miss Langley continued. "People, animals, plants—every living thing. The sooner you learn that lesson, the better off you'll be."

"But Santa Claus gave her to me and—"

"If you believe in Santa Claus, then you'll probably believe this animal will survive," Miss Langley said.

"Really?" Gracie asked, missing the point entirely.

"Carvel's a fighter," I said. "She survived once and she can do it again. And anything can happen, especially on Christmas Eve. Right, Miss Langley?"

"You, too?" Miss Langley snorted.

"Right, Miss Langley?" I repeated, stressing each word.

Poor Gracie was a blubbering mess and the damn old lady was making things worse. What Gracie needed was hope and comfort, not a lecture on harsh reality. Even I could see that and I was hardly a paragon of sensitivity. What was wrong with the old lady?

Better yet, what was wrong with me? This whole disaster was my fault. If only I had let the kitten quietly expire at the Carvel stand, none of this would have ever happened. I would be watching television and Gracie would be asleep, dreaming of Christmas presents. Instead, we were in the rundown kitchen of my avowed enemy, who was determined to make Gracie feel worse than she already did. What good had I done prolonging the life of the little cat only to have her die in Miss Langley's homemade oxygen tent? Gracie would cry for the rest of her life and she would blame me.

"Maybe the Christmas angel will save her," I said for Gracie's benefit—and mine.

"Christmas angel? That's…"

I was waiting for the word "humbug."

"Delusional," she said.

Miss Langley was a lot more modern than I had figured, but just as mean.

CHAPTER 18

Christmas Eve was wearing out when the bell rang and my mother, looking like an infuriated snowman, stomped into Miss Langley's house.

"Gracie!" she called from the front door with such force that an avalanche of snowflakes fell from her coat.

"Hi, Mommy," Gracie said in a small voice. "Are you mad at me?"

"What a question," my mother said. "Of course I'm mad at you for running away in the middle of the night and scaring me half to death. What's going on here?"

"Oh, Mommy," Gracie said, running over to her and grabbing Mom around the middle. "Only Miss Langley can save my kitty."

"Where do you get these ideas?" my mother said, genuinely baffled. "You shouldn't be pestering Miss Langley."

"She's built an oxygen tent for Carvel," Evan said excitedly. "And I made the box."

"What?"

"Come and see, Mom," Evan said, dragging Mom into the kitchen.

Through the foggy Saran Wrap, the kitten looked out of focus and unreal, like a blurry photograph. I could hear the hiss of oxygen, but Carvel made no sound and lay completely still.

"That's incredible, Frances," my mother said. "Where

did you learn to do that?"

"She's a nurse," Gracie said. "And she told me nurses help people get well, so I knew she could help Carvel and I brought her my kitty. To get well."

Miss Langley frowned and said, "I suppose I told the child too much."

"Never tell Gracie anything," Evan said. "She gets it all wrong."

"Do not," Gracie said.

"Do too."

"Children! We're going home right now and leave poor Miss Langley in peace," my mother said. "Jack, grab the kitten."

"Wait," Miss Langley said. "I don't think it is a good idea to move her, especially when it is so cold outside."

What followed was a politeness duel that would have sore amazed the fencing shepherds at The Pageant. After jockeying for position, Mom launched her world-famous "we're imposing" thrust, only to be parried by Miss Langley's disarming "you're here, you might as well stay." Mom then slashed with "but we're interrupting your Christmas" and Miss Langley countered with the plausible "I wasn't doing anything anyway" defense. Mom, who could usually out-polite Emily Post, tried all sorts of techniques and tricks, but she got nowhere with the obstinate old lady.

As I watched them dance around each other, I got the distinct impression that Miss Langley didn't want us to leave, even if she believed we would be mourning by morning. That belief was confirmed when Miss Langley went for the coup de grace: "I always say what's on my mind. If I didn't want you here, I'd throw you the hell out."

Gracie was about to make a comment, but wisely thought better of it. Correcting Miss Langley's language was not a smart move for anyone, six or sixty.

Mom bravely accepted her defeat and asked what she could do to help.

"Gracie, Jack, and Evan," Miss Langley said. "You watch the kitten and tell me if there is any change in her breathing. I'll give her some more antibiotics in an hour."

Then she went into the living room with my mother to fill her in on the kitten's condition and the vigil began. Gracie and Evan stared diligently at Carvel as if she might suddenly jump up and do a dance on the kitchen table. That kind of intense concentration wouldn't last long, I thought, and I was right. Gracie yawned and put her head in her arms, her eyelids drooping. It was an hour past her bedtime and she had had an exhausting day. Evan, however, had other ideas. He jabbed Gracie in the arm with his elbow.

"Get up," he said. "It's your kitten."

"Jack, will you make me some coffee? Daddy says it's the only thing that wakes him up," Gracie said sleepily.

"No," I said. "You're too young. Walk around for a minute or ask Miss Langley if you can take a nap somewhere. You should be asleep, anyway."

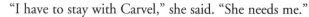

"I have to stay with Carvel," she said. "She needs me."

Gracie slid off her chair and wandered into the living room. From where I was sitting, I could see Mom and Miss Langley on the spindly sofa and, although I was not usually a snoop, I decided that listening in on their conversation was less boring that watching a motionless cat.

Gracie sat on Mom's lap and yawned, but just as she was about to drift off, she suddenly bolted upright and asked, "Mommy, why does Miss Langley have a picture of Jack?"

"That's not Jack," Miss Langley said quickly. "That's just a boy I used to know a long, long time ago."

"What's his name?" Gracie asked. "How old is he and where did you meet him? Is he coming over tonight? Can he fix cats like you?"

"Gracie, that's not polite," my mother said, attempting to pass her civility along to the next generation. "I'm sorry, Frances."

Miss Langley made the phlegmy sound but she didn't comment further.

"Put your head back down and close your eyes," my mother said to Gracie.

"No, Mommy," Gracie said. "I have to pray for Carvel. Can I have some coffee so I can stay awake?"

That was Gracie: keep asking until you got the answer you wanted.

"Certainly not," my mother said.

Disappointed, Gracie jumped off my mother's lap and came back into the kitchen to resume the watch.

I was thinking about Diane and Sally, so it didn't register on me at once, but there was a new sound coming from the oxygen tent—a ragged, desperate wheezing. Peering through the plastic, I could see that the kitten's position had changed. She had managed to get her head out of the mask.

"Go get Miss Langley," I said to Evan.

While Mom and Miss Langley fussed around the kitten, I took the opportunity to do some more snooping. I wanted to see who was in that picture. Miss Langley didn't seem like the kind of person who would snap candid shots of me putting up her Christmas lights.

I looked around the living room and saw a tarnished silver frame on a wobbly table. The guy in the picture was wearing an old-fashioned army uniform—World War I was my guess. He was standing at attention and smiling. There were no decorations on his chest, but he was wearing a single bar on his shoulder, indicating he was a lieutenant. In the background was a really cool biplane. It was difficult to tell in the faded brown-and-white photo, but I didn't think he looked anything like me. Funny, though, this was the only photograph on display in the room. Usually, people had pictures of family and friends decorating every empty space. But the rest of the place was about as personal as one of Diane's postcards.

Before they missed me, I was back in the kitchen and watched as Miss Langley placed the kitten back in the mask.

"How odd," she said. "I wouldn't have thought she could move at all."

"She's a fighter," I said. "Do you think she's getting better?"

"No," Miss Langley said. "But let's give her some more penicillin. In this case, I don't think an overdose is possible. She needs all the help she can get."

When she had finished jamming another pill down Carvel's throat, Miss Langley sighed and went back into the living room with my mother. I watched the kitten, not really seeing her, and thought about the night we had found her. Was it just a coincidence that we happened to be there or was there something else at work here?

Gracie was asleep now, dreaming of her kitten. Every few minutes she would murmur "Carvel," then drift off again. Evan, although he was struggling mightily, was losing the battle with consciousness. His chin kept dropping to his chest.

The house was dead quiet except for the hiss of the oxygen and I could hear Mom and Miss Langley talking softly. I must have dozed off myself because when I awoke they were in the middle of a conversation.

"We were to be married, you know," Miss Langley said.

"I didn't know," my mother said.

"Yes, it was 1918—a million years ago it seems—and the war looked like it would never end. Oh, how I hated that war, the death, the wounds, the disease, the hopelessness. All I could think about was peace and living a normal life. I honestly thought we were fighting the war to end all wars like they said and, after it was over, I would be married and spend the rest of my days in a little cottage somewhere taking care of my children. How stupid I was—about everything."

"Not stupid," my mother said. "Just young and inexperienced. I felt that way myself twenty-five years later during World War II. The present seemed so dismal and the future seemed so bright."

"But the future never is as bright as we hope it will be, is it?" Miss Langley said.

"Tell me about him," my mother said.

"I met him in Italy at the hospital where I was stationed with the Red Cross. He was wounded in the arm—a wound that should have ended his flying career. But he was determined to get back to his squadron and back into combat. He said he had joined the army to help his country and that his personal feelings had to wait until the war was won. I realized that if I stopped him, he would resent me forever."

"Could you have stopped him?" my mother asked.

"Almost certainly," Miss Langley said. "Things were so busy and confused at the hospital that he managed to slip away without a doctor's final release. He just put on his uniform and got a ride to his unit. Nobody there asked any questions because pilots were so desperately needed.

"I could have turned him in, I suppose, and grounded him. But I didn't. I loved him, you see, and I killed him as surely as if I had taken a gun and pulled the trigger. He was in no condition to fly a plane and he was shot down over Austrian lines. They never found him."

"You mustn't blame yourself, it was that awful war," my mother said.

"I'm sorry, I don't mean to go on," Miss Langley said softly. "I'm just an old woman spewing out her regrets on a cold Christmas Eve. But all I have left are regrets and recriminations. I've learned to live with them."

"You've learned to endure them," my mother said. "There's a difference."

Miss Langley cleared her throat and lapsed into silence. I lapsed into sleep.

I don't know how long I slept, but I was awakened by a punch in the arm. "Did you see that?" Gracie said.

"What?"

"Outside, in the playground. I think I saw Santa Claus. He waved to me," Gracie said.

"Jeez, Gracie," I groaned. "You woke me up for that?"

"But Jack, what do you think it means?" she asked, wide-eyed and awake.

"I think it means you're nuts," I said. "You know about Santa. He's an idea, an ideal, not a real person."

"Then why did he wave to me?"

"You got me there," I said, yawning.

I looked at Carvel's limp form. I couldn't detect any change, which I supposed was good. She lay on her side with her dirty cast toward me. What a wreck, I thought. She was burned and broken and drowning in her own fluids. Why didn't she just give up and die? I wondered. What kept her heart beating despite the all-out attack on her system? Was there any reason for her to survive?

This was an evening filled with questions, but no answers, and it made my head ache. I wanted to sleep, but another thought interrupted my plans. If Miss Langley thought I looked like her dead fiancé, was that the reason she was so hard on me? Did I remind her of all that was wrong in her life? That was a peculiar idea, I decided, and one I could do nothing about. If Miss Langley wanted to play the loathsome Miss Havisham, that was her business, not mine. I was no Pip. I just hoped she didn't have a bug-infested wedding cake stowed away in a cupboard.

It seemed like only a few minutes later that I heard Miss Langley whisper, "She's dead."

I opened my eyes and stared at the kitten. She hadn't moved.

"How do you know?" I asked sleepily.

"Her chest isn't moving," Miss Langley said. "I'm afraid she's gone."

"Poor little kitten," my mother said. "What a shame."

CHAPTER 19

S he's not dead! She's not dead!" Gracie cried.

"I'm sorry," Miss Langley said. "I did my best."

"No, she's got to live. Help her, Miss Langley. Please!" Gracie pleaded.

I could see the pain in the old lady's face and that surprised me. As a nurse, I assumed she had seen people die by the carload and the death of one little kitten would have no effect on her usual icy demeanor. Maybe it was Christmas, maybe it was talking about her dead fiancé, but I thought I saw real concern where nothing but contempt had existed before.

"Come on, Gracie. Let's go home. There's nothing more we can do here," my mother said. "We'll have a funeral tomorrow."

Evan and I had buried many a beloved hamster, goldfish, and guinea pig with elaborate ceremony in the backyard. Their homemade tombstones still decorated a portion of the yard.

"No!" Gracie screamed. "I won't leave her!"

Then she did something she hadn't done in years. She threw herself to the cold linoleum floor and pitched a first-class fit. I was embarrassed. Gracie was much too old for that sort of childish behavior, but I suppose she just couldn't let go.

"Jack, pick her up," my mother said. "I'm sorry about this, Frances. I know you did everything you could."

I grabbed Gracie and held her close to me, trying to smother her and stop her from kicking me. But it was like holding onto a bag of particularly angry eels. She twisted and struggled, attempting to get away.

"Miss Langley!" Gracie screamed in a voice filled such despair that it made the hairs on the back of my neck stand up.

"Wait!" Miss Langley said suddenly. "There's only one thing I can think of to do."

She untaped the oxygen tent and brought the inert kitten out in her hand. Carvel's eyes were closed, but the look of pain on her face had gone. She looked peaceful and at rest. I could see no sign of breathing or any other movement.

Miss Langley placed the kitten on the table and thumped her on the chest with two fingers. No reaction. Then she repeated the action twice more and was rewarded with a gasping breath from the kitten. Carvel coughed and expelled some greenish liquid. She opened her eyes in surprise, then closed them again. But at least she was breathing.

"See?" Gracie said through her tears. "I knew she wasn't dead."

"What did you do?" my mother asked.

"I got her heart started again," Miss Langley said. "It doesn't always work and her heart may stop again at any minute. But we may have bought a little more time for the penicillin to get to work."

I put Gracie down and she went right to Carvel, bending down and kissing the kitten.

"I knew you would be okay," she said. "Santa said so."

This time Miss Langley's face didn't twist into a sneer. She smiled at Gracie and said, "At this point, I'm willing to believe anything."

"It's a Christmas miracle," my mother said.

Mom thought everything was a Christmas miracle, but I still wasn't convinced. Besides, Carvel was a long way from being cured. I looked at the clock. It was after six. We had been at this for nine long hours and I was starving. I was going to say something, but I figured Miss Langley was not about to feed us.

"Anybody hungry?" Miss Langley said. "I've got some eggs and I can make toast."

"Can I have some coffee?" Gracie asked.

"No, dear," she said in a kindly voice.

I couldn't help thinking that if I had asked, Miss Langley would have yelled at me. But I was willing to eat anything she put on a plate. I moved the kitten's oxygen tent to a spare kitchen chair and we sat down.

"What do we do now?" my mother asked.

"We wait to see if the kitten keeps on breathing," Miss Langley said. "We'll give her a couple of hours; then I think we ought to get her to the animal hospital, even if it is Christmas Day. There's sure to be somebody on duty who is more competent than I."

"I don't believe that's possible. But it's too bad that we have to give the kitten away," my mother said. "After all you've done."

"What?" Miss Langley said. "How can you do that?"

"Carvel makes Daddy sick," Gracie said sadly. "But I know who would like her."

"Who?" Miss Langley asked.

"You," Gracie said. "She's your Christmas present."

Miss Langley shook her head.

"You've got to take her," Gracie said. "Santa waved to me, so you have to do it."

"With a recommendation like that, how can you say no?" my mother asked.

"I don't want the responsibility," Miss Langley said tightly.

"You *are* responsible for saving Carvel's life," my mother said. "She belongs to you now. Besides, cats are not much trouble. Have you ever owned one before?"

"In Italy, there was a little calico cat that used to come by my quarters. I would always put out a bowl of milk, but I can't say I owned him," Miss Langley said.

"Nobody has ever owned a cat," my mother said. "They own you, Frances, and you're stuck."

Gracie jumped off her chair, ran over to Miss Langley, and hugged her with such strength that she almost knocked the old lady to the floor.

"Oh, thank you, thank you," Gracie said. "I knew you'd take care of her. I love you."

Miss Langley looked stunned, but she patted Gracie on the head and looked to my mother for guidance.

"Consider yourself owned," my mother said with a smile.

✳ 🔔 ✳

By the time we returned from the animal hospital, Carvel was pumped full of antibiotics and breathing regularly. She opened her eyes and meowed, causing Gracie and Miss Langley to fall all over themselves to pet her and whisper words of encouragement. Not that Carvel needed much encouragement. She was, without a doubt, the toughest cat in the world. Although she had probably lost eight of her nine lives, she was still alive. I had to admire her persistence and I was glad we had rescued her.

Mom invited Miss Langley for Christmas dinner, but she declined, saying she thought she should keep an eye on the kitten. I was impressed into the ambulance corps and was told to be on twenty-four hour alert in case Carvel needed to be ferried back to the hospital. I was kind of hoping for a chance to wheel the Chrysler through the snow, but the call never came. Miss Langley was a more than competent nurse.

Christmas dinner, it turned out, was grilled cheese sandwiches because Mom had forgotten to defrost the turkey. Nobody seemed to mind, but Mom was grateful Miss Langley had decided not to come over. That would have been too embarrassing, she said.

Almost as an afterthought, we opened our presents. Mom was appropriately appalled by the giant orange ashtray that I had commissioned for her. The look on her face was worth every one of the hundred cents I had invested in it.

"You didn't really make this, did you Jack?" Mom asked, clearly horrified that her sixteen-year-old-son potted like a nine-year-old.

"Don't you like it?" I said, trying to sound offended by her cold reception of my lavish gift of fired clay.

"I think it would make a wonderful pen holder," my father said, pointing to the single, small opening in the pumpkin-like object. "Except that it would probably break the desk."

"You don't like it," I said, my lower lip trembling like Gracie's when she was about to cry. "But you always said you liked homemade presents."

"Uh, well, that is—"

"I like it, Jack," Gracie said, jumping into an awkward situation. "Can I keep it in my room? What is it?"

I milked the joke for as long as I could, then produced the backup present I had bought.

"Wise guy," my mother said, but she laughed.

After Gracie had slipped off to visit Carvel and Miss Langley, I sat on the couch and stared at the battered tree. It had been a long night and day and I was still reeling from the experience. I was not sure what exactly had happened, other than the obvious, but I was convinced something extraordinary had occurred. Thoughts of Carvel, Miss Langley, and Gracie kept invading my mind. I was so deep in thought, I didn't hear Mom come into the room.

"Did you have a good Christmas?" she asked, sitting down next to me.

"'Good' wouldn't be the word I'd use," I said. "But at least Gracie and Carvel managed to live through it."

"Barely," my mother said. "Poor Miss Langley."

"I've been thinking, Mom," I said. "Why didn't she ever get married?"

"I guess she was afraid," Mom said. "She didn't want to put herself through the pain again."

"She was scared?" I asked. "That's hard to believe. She's tougher than Carvel."

"That may be," Mom said. "But everyone has to make up his own mind about what love means to them. There's no right or wrong way to love. And there are all kinds of love. Look at Gracie. In her short life she has never loved anything as much as Carvel, but I would be willing to bet that in ten years she'll have some dopey boyfriend she thinks is the only guy in the world for her. Ten years after that, if she's lucky, she'll find someone she wants to marry."

"So, there's no timetable or plan to follow?" I asked.

"Have you ever seen pictures of Cupid?" my mother said. "You know, the little guy with the bow and arrow? Well, love is like being ambushed. Just when you think you're safe, Cupid pops out of the bushes and lets you have it right through the heart."

"But that never happened to Miss Langley again?"

"No, she wouldn't allow it. She hid herself away and she was darn good at it. Love never found her again," my mother said.

"Until now, maybe," I said. "Even if it is only a kitten."

"Perhaps," my mother said. "Love is strange and mysterious. It's what keeps life exciting and interesting."

I thought about what she said and decided that I would never fall in love like that. I didn't want to pine away for a lost love when there were girls like Sally Preston around. That would have been a waste.

"Thanks, Mom," I said, getting up.

"Oh, Jack," my mother called after me. "Will you go get Gracie? I don't want her out after dark."

"She did pretty well last night," I said, reluctant to go back out into the cold.

"Please, Jack," she said. "It's Christmas Day."

"Yeah, I know," I said.

As I trod the well-worn path to Miss Langley's house, I didn't know if I was any wiser about the mysteries of love, but I did learn one thing: I didn't know as much as I thought I did only a few days ago. I had entirely misread Miss Langley, I had underestimated my parents, and I had scoffed at Gracie's unshakable faith. The last was perhaps the most shocking, but Carvel's survival, I was sure now, had less to do with Miss Langley's skills as a nurse and more to do with a little girl's prayers.

Mrs. Langley opened the door and said, "Oh, it's you."

I guess she was expecting the President of the United States or St. Nicholas, because I didn't seem to be high on her list of expected visitors.

"You'd better come in then," she said.

"How's the kitten?" I asked.

"She's doing remarkably well," Miss Langley said, her face suddenly becoming animated. "Her heartbeat is regular, her lungs are draining, and she doesn't have too much trouble breathing."

"Great," said. "I'm here to take Gracie home."

"Can't I stay a few more minutes?" Gracie called from the kitchen. "We're going to see if Carvel will eat her dinner."

"All right," I said. "But then we've got to go."

I took off my coat and followed Miss Langley down the narrow hallway to the kitchen, where I found the kitten lying in the box I had made for her. The plastic and coat hangers had been removed and Carvel was resting on a piece of pink satin comforter. Her eyes were open and she seemed interested in what the three of us were doing. She didn't move much, but she kept looking around the room nervously, as if she knew something was up.

"I've heated up some milk," Miss Langley said. "Let's see if she'll take some."

Deftly, Miss Langley produced an eyedropper from her apron and dipped it in the warm milk. Then she put it to the kitten's mouth and squeezed the red rubber bulb. The milk spurted out, but Carvel ignored it, not even licking up the remains with her tongue.

"Gracie, hold her mouth open and we'll try again," Miss Langley said.

Gracie did as she was told and this time Miss Langley shot the milk directly down the cat's throat.

Carvel stumbled to her feet and screeched, coughing the milk back up and looking at us as if we were trying to poison her.

"I don't think she likes it," Gracie said.

"You think?" I said.

"She has to get something in her," Miss Langley said. "She needs liquids and nutrients to survive."

"I've got an idea," I said. "Carvel's never been much of a milk or water drinker, but there's one thing she really loves."

"Pea juice!" Gracie said. "There's some in the bag Mommy gave me for Miss Langley."

"What are you talking about, child?" Miss Langley asked.

"When she was sick before, Jack gave her pea juice and she really, really liked it," Gracie said enthusiastically.

Miss Langley shrugged and shook her head.

I opened the brown paper bag and found three cans of the expensive peas among the packets of dry cat food.

"Just open a can," I said. "And give her an eyedropperful of the juice. She won't eat the peas themselves."

Miss Langley made her phlegmy sound, but managed to overcome her better judgement and soon had the eyedropper poised at the kitten's mouth. Carvel shook her head, stared at us angrily, and even hissed as menacingly as she could.

"She's mad now, Jack." Gracie said.

"Why don't you talk to her?" I asked.

Miss Langley looked at me as if I had suddenly gone loony.

"Put her in your lap and tell her how important it is for her to drink something," I continued, ignoring the old lady's skeptical stare.

Gracie hauled the kitten from the box and held her. She stared into the kitten's gold-green eyes and said, "I love you, Carvel. You are my bestest friend in the whole wide world and you've been real sick. I want you to get better so we can play like we used to in the fort, except this time I'll play with you at Miss Langley's house instead so Daddy won't get sick anymore. Do you understand?"

Carvel looked at Gracie quizzically as if she were trying to analyze the torrent of words.

"We will have so much fun," Gracie continued. "And we can have tea parties and play dress-up and hide-and-seek, you'll really like that, and we will go for rides in Jack's car, and play on the lawn, and go shopping."

Carvel sneezed. I guess she didn't like shopping.

"But you have to drink your pea juice so you'll get all better and be able to play with me. Just drink a little bit. It's delicious. For me, please?"

The kitten stared at Gracie intently, as if she were trying to make up her mind; then she meowed softly.

"She says it's okay now," Gracie said with complete confidence.

Miss Langley had a strange look on her face, but she handed Gracie the eyedropper, and stood back to watch.

"Here you go," Gracie said.

Without hesitation, Carvel began to lap at the tip of the eyedropper.

"Slowly squeeze some into her mouth," Miss Langley said.

Gracie did as she was told and in seconds had emptied the contents into Carvel's mouth. The kitten swallowed every bit and mewed for more. Miss Langley gladly complied, watching in fascination as Gracie fed the kitten dropper after dropper of green liquid.

"I've never heard of such a thing," Miss Langley said. "Who would have thought a kitten would prefer pea juice to milk?"

"Carvel's not your average cat," I said.

I was going to tell her that it wasn't the pea juice that made the kitten eat. It was the person on the other end of the eyedropper—Gracie. Watching my little sister carefully and gently feed the kitten, all the while murmuring soft words of encouragement, confirmed my suspicions that Gracie had some sort of extraordinary connection with the ragged ball of orange fur. She really believed Santa had given Carvel to her and that it was her duty to save the kitten—even if she had to give her away.

Miss Langley, too, seemed to sense something because she pursed her lips and began pacing the floor as if she wanted to ask a question, but didn't dare. Every few steps, she would stop and stare at Gracie and Carvel, then resume her distracted walk.

When Carvel stopped feeding, I picked her up and put her back in the box. She fell asleep instantly.

"She'll be all right now," Gracie said. "Can I come over in the morning to feed her again?"

"Of course," Miss Langley said. "Anytime you want. And I mean that sincerely."

Gracie took my hand and we walked home slowly through the crusty snow. We were almost there when Gracie asked me, "Did I do the right thing, Jack? Giving Carvel to Miss Langley, I mean."

"Face it, Gracie, you didn't have a choice. But, yes, you did the right thing. If Carvel was a gift to you from Santa, maybe he meant for you to give her to Miss Langley all along. Miss Langley doesn't drive, so she would have never found the kitten and saved her like you did. I think you gave Miss Langley the greatest gift she ever received. Carvel was the perfect Christmas present—only she had the wrong address label on her."

"Miss Langley loves Carvel almost as much as me," Gracie said. "But what about if—"

"No more questions," I said, opening the door to our house. "It's way past your bedtime. Just say good night, Gracie."

"Good night, Gracie," she giggled.

EPILOGUE

The marmalade cat sat on the old lady's lap absently cleaning her sleek fur and purring softly. Her thoughts were of the little one who would come to play with her soon, as she did most afternoons. The cat looked forward to batting the ball of yarn and being chased and pestered for an hour or so, but mostly she was grateful for the peace and quiet that surrounded her.

Fortunately, the old lady was much gentler, stroking her only occasionally, but allowing the cat to nest in her lap any time she wanted. She had found warmth and security there during the cold winter months, and now that the days were longer and the weather was warmer, she saw no reason to abandon her preferred roost.

She had grown used to the serenity of her new home and that suited her. She yawned and stretched and settled down. The only sounds she heard were the ticking of a clock, the rustle of pages as the old lady read her book, and the noise of the children playing outside.

Sometimes, when the old lady was in another room, the cat would sit on the sill of the kitchen window and watch the birds circle and swoop over the playground. She wasn't quite sure what they were, but they fascinated her with their acrobatic movements. With her right paw, she would swipe at them, but they never got close enough for her to reach.

Thoughts of her abused past had dimmed and she no

longer felt the shadow of illness pressing down on her. In fact, she was as well as she could remember. The old lady fed her twice a day and never forgot. And she always had plenty of the succulent green juice that she craved. Her left leg sometimes got stiff when it rained, but usually she didn't notice the slight limp when she walked. It had long since stopped hurting her.

The cat licked her paw and was rubbing her face when a sudden noise shattered two panes of glass and her tranquility. She sprang up from the old lady's lap, back arched, fur erect, ready to fight an unseen enemy. Hissing and spitting, she leaped from her perch and ran to the small space between the stove and the counter for protection.

Peering warily from her fort, the cat watched as the old lady slowly got up from her chair, pursed her lips, and walked to the window. She looked out through the smashed panes and shook her head. From below came a chorus of young voices shouting, "Sorry, Miss Langley."

Then she bent over painfully and picked up the dirty round ball that had come flying through the glass. She hefted it in her hand for a minute before throwing it back to the playground through the jagged hole it had made.

"Thanks, Miss Langley," the children called in unison.

The cat watched curiously as the old lady cleaned up the shards of glass scattered around the kitchen. When it looked safe, she limped out from her hiding place by the stove, jumped gracefully into the old lady's lap, and began to purr. Although the cat couldn't see her face, the old lady smiled broadly and, for a moment, cast the years away.

JOHN S. LITTELL

is the author of several books, including *French Impressions* and *Susie, Sadly, and the Black Torpedo of Doom*. He is a former publishing executive and lives in New York City.